SET UP

A Second Chance Small Town Novel

KELLY COLLINS

Copyright © 2016 by Kelly Collins

No part of this publication may be reproduced, distributed, or transmitted in any form or by any means, including photocopying, recording, or other electronic or mechanical methods, without the prior written permission of the publisher, except as permitted by U.S. copyright law. For permission requests, contact kelly@authorkellycollins.com.

The story, all names, characters, and incidents portrayed in this production are fictitious. No identification with actual persons (living or deceased), places, buildings, and products is intended or should be inferred. All products or brand names are trademarks of their respective owners.

Dedication

To my family, who have never doubted me for a second.

Chapter 1

NATALIE

Diamonds are a girl's best friend…so they say. That's true until they're analyzed, picked apart, and declared flawed—or jailed for grand larceny.

"Natalie Diamond. I can't believe they're letting you go."

Officer Ellis stood behind the out-processing counter and greeted me with a beer belly and tobacco-stained smile.

"You're going to miss me."

All I had to do was flash my ten-carat smile and lean in their direction, and the other guards were charmed—but not Officer Ellis; he didn't fall for a peek of cleavage. Of course, with a prison-issued bra, a girl couldn't get the lift it took to gain the notice she deserved, but a nice word and smile could gain you favor, and favor was what you wanted when you were stuck in a cellblock with a bunch of bitches.

Officer Ellis always had a smile to share.

He licked his sausage-like fingers and shuffled through a stack of papers two inches thick until he found the one with my name typed across the top. "In the grand scheme of things, you were easy, young lady."

"Now, Officer Ellis, don't be starting rumors about me."

He shook his head with fatherly disapproval and slapped my exit form on the counter. "Honey, I don't need to start rumors about you. The whole place has been buzzing with them for years." He rocked back and forth while he tapped the computer keyboard with furious urgency.

I'd given the guards a run for their money, but I'd been taught to make my mark on society. There was no way to leave here and not be a legend. I was Natalie Diamond, and that meant I was made to sparkle.

"How fast can you spring me from this joint?"

"You in a hurry?" His pudgy digits raced over the keyboard. With that much movement, his fingers should be thin and sleek, but Officer Ellis' wife loved to bake, and he loved to eat. On occasion, my brand of sparkle would earn me a double chocolate brownie.

"Yes." I pulled at the pencil skirt three seasons out of fashion and tighter than a pair of Spanx. Those brownies had not been my friend. Sweets managed to go straight to my ass.

"Big date?" There was that fatherly look again—the one that pulled an honest answer straight from my soul.

"As a matter of fact, I'm going to see Mickey, Holly, and Megan."

He growled something inaudible. "That has trouble written all over it." He cleared his throat. "I better not see you in here again. Your dad might be gone, but if you show up in my cell block again, I'll stand in for him and turn you over my knee."

"Oh, Officer Ellis." I lowered my head and lifted my eyes. "Don't tease me." Coy was a hard look to pull off when my face was free of make-up. A girl was supposed to look through the fringe of her lashes to set the tone, but Maybelline hadn't made its way to the commissary of this facility.

"Natalie, get your life together. Figure out who you are."

A female officer entered through a side door and plopped a plastic bag on the counter, then turned and walked back through the same door without a word or a look. To her I was invisible. A number. A nobody. One fewer body to cavity search.

"I'm whoever I need to be. That's the best way to be in order to survive in this world. Today I'm a Diamond, and I have those four *C*s in my pocket. I'm the epitome of quality."

That line was my mantra. One that had been played on repeat my entire life. *Believe it and conceive it,* my mother always said, but believing and conceiving didn't make it true—it just perpetuated whatever lie was being told.

Officer Ellis' laugh echoed off the faded gray walls. "You've got the four *C*s down all right. Cute. Cunning. Creative. Chameleon."

Yep, Officer Ellis had me pegged. That's probably why I liked him so much. He saw me for who I wasn't. During my lifetime of twenty-five years, I had tried on more personas than an A-list actor, but in the past three, I had never fooled him.

I plucked a behavior straight from my fussy teen arsenal and rolled my eyes skyward. "You're such a comedian."

He stamped the outtake form with the date and opened the plastic bag, dumping all the contents on the counter.

"Look through it and sign here." He pointed to the bottom of the page.

I signed without looking. It didn't matter whether everything was there. What I had was three years old and in dire need of replacement. But my heart skipped a beat when the gold tube of Cardinal Sin lipstick rolled toward me, begging to be applied. A signature color was important branding for a girl. If you had to be known for something, red lipstick was a start. A turn of the cylinder and stroke across my dry lips, and suddenly I felt more like myself. It was funny how the cloak of a little lipstick could make me feel authentic.

I reached inside the Coach bag, and my fingers brushed against a slim piece of fabric. It was still there. My heart leapt.

I pulled the red satin ribbon out and curled it in my palm. My mind reached back to before this terrible, cold, gray place to before the bad decision, to before my path went left instead of right.

To when my father was still alive. I could see him, on his knees before eight-year-old me, sliding the ribbon off the box and tying it to my wrist.

Be a good girl, sweetheart, and good things will happen.

I'd kept the ribbon all these years. A reminder, a talisman. For a long time, I'd lost track of the message in that slender scrap, but now I vowed, as I looped the frayed ribbon around my wrist, now I would remember.

Be a good girl, sweetheart, and good things will happen.

I needed some good in my life.

"I'm serious, Natalie. I don't want to see you back here." Office Ellis' voice was tinged with warmth and sadness. He once said I reminded him of his daughter. She was a lucky girl to have him for a father. He was a simple man, but a good man. It showed in his belly laughs and gifted brownies.

I stood tall and gave him a salute. "Yes, sir, but if I were to come back, just know it wouldn't be because I stole my own stuff and got caught doing it."

"Yeah, yeah, three years later, and you're still claiming innocence." He tucked the completed form into a drawer beneath the computer screen.

"No, I took it, but I was taking something that rightly belonged to me."

He shook his head. "Keep telling yourself lies, and you'll always be imprisoned, whether it's here or in your head." He pointed to the door. "You staying or going?"

"Going." I shoved the rest of my stuff into my bag and waited like a child to be dismissed.

"Get the hell out of my prison, Natalie Diamond, and never come back. You're better than this place. Find your purpose."

"My purpose begins with a trip to Cherry Creek Mall. I'm going shopping." I knew my strengths. That was something I could be a very good girl at.

Another shake of his head, and he pushed the button that opened the door to my future. My heart hammered when I touched the handle. What was waiting outside? My mother, I hoped, or maybe her driver, or Rosa the housekeeper. Mickey had offered to pick me up, but I needed to clear the air with my mother. I'd sent her my release date and time weeks ago; surely, she'd be here.

In a hurry to be free, I pushed the door and swung it wide open,

Set Up

hitting the metal rail behind it. It popped back, and if not for quick reflexes, I would have been knocked flat on my butt.

Spring air whipped around me, fresh and crisp. Off to my right was the yard, the place I'd spent most mornings and late afternoons dreaming of freedom. I breathed deep. It was the same air, but somehow today smelled different. Freedom carried its own scent.

The sun sat high on the horizon. Streams of light pierced my eyes like lasers. Squinting through the glare, I searched the parking lot for a familiar face or car, but only an old, beat-up brown sedan was present.

I swallowed the lump of despair lodged in my throat and searched the area one more time, hoping I'd missed something. At the bottom of the steps stood a little blonde girl dressed in a pink tutu and shiny black shoes. One look at me, and her bright smile curled south into a frown.

"It's not her, Grandma." She stomped her Mary Janes and crossed her arms over a T-shirt that read 'Mama's Girl' in purple glitter.

"She's comin', baby. We're early." The older woman tugged at the little girl's pigtails.

"We should have brought her flowers."

Her little voice fell with every word, like somehow her presence would be less if she didn't bring gifts. Maybe that was my problem. Would Mom have shown up if gifts were promised? I was the damn gift. Didn't she understand that?

"We can't afford flowers, honey. We was lucky to get here at all." The older woman looked back at the brown car held together by body shop putty and duct tape.

Slumped against her grandmother, Little Miss Sunshine sighed. The breeze carried her disappointment to my ears.

I made my way down the metal stairs, taking each step carefully so I didn't catch a heel in the grate. When I got to the bottom, I stood in front of the munchkin.

Her head tilted back until her blue eyes stared into mine. "Do you know my mommy?"

"Who's your mommy?"

I looked past her and craned my neck in the direction of the road. Nothing. Not even a wisp of dust lifted in the distance.

"Del White." She said the name with pride, like everyone should know her mom.

It didn't sound familiar, but there were hundreds of inmates, and it was hard to be sure. "Sorry, I don't recognize that name." I looked over my shoulder toward the metal door. "It could be a while. The system works on its own time, but she'll be here." A little smile tipped the edge of her mouth. "I heard you talk about flowers." I looked to the right, where wildflowers danced in the breeze against the yard fence.

"I wanted flowers for Mommy, but we can't get 'em." Her little shoulders sagged like a tired old woman's.

"This could be your lucky day." I pegged Grandma with a look and nodded toward the fence. "Can we?"

Once she acquiesced, I held out my hand, and a sticky little palm slipped into it. "How old are you?" She lifted her free hand and showed me five fingers. "Wow, five. You're almost old enough to drive."

She giggled and skipped while I struggled to walk in my four-inch heels. It was bad enough that I was out of practice, but with all the holes and pebbles in my path, I was lucky to stay on my feet and not face plant onto the asphalt.

Grandma followed closely behind, not taking her eyes off little blondie. She didn't need to worry—the little girl was darling, but if I were going back to prison, it wouldn't be for kidnapping.

"Oooh," the little sprite whispered when she noticed the wild daisies growing along the chain-link fence.

"Go wild, little one."

I let go of her hand and stood back. She raced ahead and danced along the prison enclosure, picking the white and yellow flowers without reserve. When she finished, she had no less than a dozen stems spilling from her hands.

She struggled with the bundle, which needed something to bind the stems together.

"What's your name?"

"Emily."

"Well, Emily, take a look around and see if you can find a hair tie or a ribbon."

A brief glance around the parking lot came up empty. The little girl's eyes zoomed in on the red ribbon I'd wrapped around my wrist.

"Not this one, honey. It's my lucky ribbon." I rubbed the frayed satin.

"What makes it lucky?" She was as cute as one of those little capuchin monkeys—the ones that steal your heart—then your wallet.

"It was given to me by someone I love."

"Emily, we better let this woman get on her way." Grandma bent over to pick up several dropped flowers.

Those two were a pair. They could've made a mint on any corner with a sign that said, "I'm cute—give me whatever you got." Only, this little girl wasn't asking for anything. All she wanted was to show her mom she loved her by giving her a bunch of hand-picked daisies that would be withered and dead within an hour.

I took one last look at my lucky ribbon. It was a child's reminder of the love of a parent now gone. Did I need a reminder of Daddy's love? At twenty-five, did I need his memory telling me to behave? I'd lived without it for the past three years; surely, I'd survive now. Besides, it hadn't been lucky for me when I got arrested, but maybe Emily would feel lucky to receive it.

I slid my fingers over it one last time and said a silent *I love you* to my father before I unfastened it. "Now it's your lucky ribbon. Take care of it, okay?"

With great attention to detail, I tied the perfect bow around the stems. Emily's gap-toothed smile made another appearance, and I knew I'd made the right decision. To me, it was a reminder of the past. To Emily, it was a harbinger of her future—an offering to her mother that contained dreams of a new life, and I hoped it was a happy one.

"Thank you."

She brought the daisies to her nose and inhaled. If her grin was any indication, they didn't smell like dirt the way I imagined. Emily's smile made it look like they were scented with sugar and hope.

Just then, the metal door to the prison swung open and that little blonde monkey bounded away from me and into the arms of her mother.

It didn't take much for them to race to the beat-up car and zoom away, leaving me alone and wondering why my mother didn't love me enough to show up.

Chapter 2

NATALIE

In the distance, a dust cloud followed Emily and her family down the desolate road. Alone, I sat on the metal stairs and dug through my purse for change. The payphone to the right stood like a bully beside me, mocking me for having so much and so little at the same time. Where were the people who said they would always be my friends? Where were the men who had declared their undying love while my credit cards were active and my bank account was full? Where in the hell was my mother when I needed her the most?

I scraped enough change together and wobbled my way to the phone, only to find it out of order. The universe hated me, or maybe it was only my mother.

The reason was obvious. Marla wasn't interested in a diamond with flaws.

Just as I climbed to the top of the steps and fisted up to knock on the worn metal door, a horn pierced the air. In a move better left to stuntmen, the approaching blue truck spun in a circle and came to a stop at the bottom of the steps. Mickey jumped out.

I had never been more grateful to see a person in my life. Just a few more seconds, and I would have been pounding on the prison door, begging to be let back in—if only to make a phone call.

"What are you doing here?" I tottered down the steps for the second time and managed to stay upright until Mickey plowed me over with an exuberant hug. If not for her open door, we would have fallen to the ground instead of the cab. "Oh my God, you have no idea what a savior you are."

"I've got some idea." Mickey looked to the top of the stairs and waved. I followed her line of sight straight to Officer Ellis, who filled the doorway.

"He called you?"

"Yes, he said you were alone and looked like an unclaimed orphan. He also threatened to have you arrested for loitering if someone didn't pick you up soon."

"That would be my luck."

Reflexively, I reached down to touch my ribbon before I remembered it was gone. I waved to the old man, who stood where he belonged, on a pedestal above me. He gave me a curt nod and walked back inside the door.

"Get in the truck."

"Gladly." It wasn't the Town Car I expected. This was better because the driver of the truck loved me.

Seconds later, we were tearing out of the parking lot like Bonnie and Clyde after a heist.

"No Mom, huh?"

"Nope." The impact of her question hit me. I blinked back tears. Weren't moms supposed to be there no matter what? Weren't they supposed to fight for their young, like animals did in the wild? "She can't avoid me forever."

Mickey changed the subject, for which I was grateful. "Turn around and watch the past fade before your eyes. You'll never be here again—unless, of course, you have to pick up Robyn—then you'll see it one more time. The view is so much better from this side of the fence."

Dirt and tumbleweeds blended with the old truck's exhaust. The

Set Up

guard towers shrank until they disappeared, along with the past several years of my life.

"That's a beautiful sight to see."

I had a love/hate relationship with the prison. I hated the confinement, the lack of choices, and the reason I was there. But I loved the people who saw value in me—the guards who were nice to me and the girls who had become my family. Without Mickey, Holly, Megan, and Robyn, I would have perished.

We all brought something to the table. Mickey was the trusting one; Holly, the smart one; Megan, the vulnerable one. Robyn was tough, and I was comic relief. We all had our roles in prison, and we played them well.

"Where to?"

"Home."

Mickey stopped the truck on the soft shoulder of the empty two-lane highway. "The ranch or your mom's?" She wanted me to call the ranch home. It was part of her grand scheme to get all the girls from Cell Block C to her place. She gave me those damn puppy dog eyes, which were unnecessary because I had nowhere else to go. I didn't see myself as a girl who lived at a ranch, but homelessness looked less appealing than horseshit and hay.

"Mickey, you have no idea how much I appreciate everything you're doing for me. The last time I was at a ranch, it was up in Big Sky, Montana, and there was a butler and a spa. I'm not sure I'm ranch material, but I am grateful to have a place to go."

Mickey laughed. "We have something similar. There's a lot of butts, but no lers. They're mostly horse's asses. However, there is some fine man flesh. We also have several water troughs, not quite the spa experience, but nice to dip in when the summer sun beats down."

"I'll keep that in mind."

"Good. Your cabin is ready. The girls were putting on the finishing touches when I left. They put you in cabin number one, knowing you'd settle for nothing less."

Mickey turned onto the highway and headed south. It was the

opposite direction of where I'd been raised and in fact seemed appropriate—like I was heading straight for hell.

"I don't need to be number one. They make me sound like such a diva. I'm not that bad."

"Puh-lease. You're worse, but we love you anyway."

"You better because you guys might be the only ones who love me." I laid my head against the cool window and watched the landscape whiz by.

"Forget about your mom tonight. We have celebrating to do. You can deal with it tomorrow."

She was right. This situation with Mom needed a quick resolution, but I also needed to give myself a little bit of time to cool off and get my bearings.

"Rick's Roost tonight at six, right?" That was what she'd said the last time we chatted.

"Yes. Everyone from the ranch will be there. None of the hands would miss another homecoming since they eat and drink for free." She gave me a sardonic smile. "Plus, I make it a requirement."

It was amazing to see how much Mickey had grown as a woman. When I'd first met her, she was a gullible young girl. Now she was a woman who ran a ranch and ruled men.

"How many of those cowboys are single?"

I ran my fingers over the pink silk shirt I was arrested in, its softness a foreign feeling after the three years of a polyester/cotton blend.

"You girls are snapping them up faster than I can hire them. We have Cole and Tyson, and there's a new ranch hand named Toby, but he's too young for you. All the rest are McKinleys, and they're taken. Roland's around, and he's a really nice guy."

"Oh lord, the nice guy label. You realize describing him as a nice guy is like telling an obese woman she has a pretty face. It's a way to overlook everything else."

"He is a nice guy. Kind of like a brother to everyone. In fact, he might as well be a McKinley because he spends enough time with them to be considered a sibling."

"Mark him off the list. 'Nice guy' and 'brother material' don't

Set Up

fall within my preferred proclivities." I picked at a hangnail. *What's the chance I can get a pedicure and manicure within the week?* I really needed to get this stuff straightened out with Mom soon, or the only thing I'd be looking to get was a job, and they didn't come easy to ex-convicts. "Are any of them fuckable?"

Mickey shook her head. "It's still about the orgasms for you."

"What?"

"Nothing. Someday, you're going to look beyond your personal needs and consider someone else's."

"Aww, are you saying there's hope for me yet?"

Mickey rocked her head from shoulder to shoulder. "Maybe. If it were up to me, I'd put you in cabin six, but the girls said no. Everyone who stays there gets hooked up or knocked up. Both scenarios require an intimacy you've yet to embrace."

"Remind me to hug the girls."

"Remind yourself, we're almost there." She downshifted and turned onto a dirt road. The truck moaned and hissed until she found the right gear.

"Why do you drive this old thing? Can't you afford a better one?"

"It serves its purpose. When it no longer does, I'll make a change."

We drove under a sign decorated with Mickey's moniker. *M and M Ranch* was emblazoned across the top. Hanging below was a smaller sign that read *Second Chance Ranch*. This was Mickey's personal halfway house. What a strange transition for me. I'd been a debutante, then a prisoner; I wasn't sure whether the ranch was a step up or down. My guess was down—I seemed to be on an endless plunging slope.

Up ahead, the scene unfolded like a modern-day Western. Cowboys and horses walked the grounds. Big pickup trucks and trailers filled the parking lot. A large house sat to the right, looking over eight smaller children that dotted the landscape ahead. Little cabins that screamed *country* and *salt of the earth*. Two concepts I had never grasped. I was Prada, not paddocks. Harrods, not horseshit.

I was right. I'd traveled south straight into hell.

"You need to change your clothes." Mickey turned briefly and looked me up and down. "Megan and Holly put some things in your closet. It's part of the Second Chance Ranch reintegration program."

Now it made sense as to why they had been hounding me about my favorite colors and clothing size. "Really? They shopped for me?" The thought terrified and charmed me all at once.

"Yep. Holly also put a bunch of her stuff in your closet. Now that she's preggers, she can't fit into anything."

We rolled to a stop between the house and the big red barn.

"Now get out of my truck. I've got shit to do."

"Love you, too."

I reached inside myself to find Annie Oakley, but the minute I opened the door, Calamity Jane made her presence known. The heel of my shoe caught on the lip of the floorboard and sent me hurtling to the ground. Gravel bit into my palms and knees. I swallowed my tears and bounced back to my feet, hoping no one witnessed my arrival. I'd spent years in prison without shedding a tear—I wasn't going to break that streak today. Diamonds didn't cry. They were hard and firm in their resolve and twinkled under the dimmest light. Today, I would twinkle.

Leaning forward, I took a cursory look. Not too bad considering how much it hurt. My knees were scratched, and my skirt was split clear up my thigh. Bent over and waiting was at the top of my recent sexual fantasies, but in my version there was a naked man behind me, not an old blue truck.

Black boots came into view. Strong hands gripped my arms to steady me. A Nordic god faced me. His smile mocked me. "I'd give you a ten for the dismount, but a two for the landing. Are you okay?" His voice dripped with sex appeal—thick and sweet like honey. My knees wobbled.

"Yes." I brushed my hands across my skirt, leaving streaks of blood on the fabric. "I think." Picking out an embedded pebble from my pinkie finger, I winced.

Mickey rounded the truck and rushed to my side. "Shit, Natalie. Are you okay?" I didn't look at her. In fact, I lifted my bloody palm and shooed her away. The only face I wanted to see was in front of me.

My real-life Thor seemed to sense this. "Hey, Mick, I got this," he said in a slow, sexy drawl. "Cole needs to talk to you about something in the barn."

Mickey hovered for all of a second. "All right. Clean her up and take her to cabin one. I'll be there in ten." She walked away, singing "Another One Bites the Dust." I wasn't sure whether she was referring to my fall from the truck or my falling immediately for this gorgeous man.

He turned my hands over and inspected my palms. "You'll live, but we should get you cleaned up."

I nodded but stayed silent. Not because I didn't have anything to say, but because his presence made me speechless.

He leaned over and inspected my knees. With a slow whistle that vibrated straight to my lady bits, he said, "You'll be feeling that for days." All I could think was, *God, I hope so*. Then I realized he wasn't referring to the ache between my legs.

I'd never felt better until I looked down and saw what he saw. Blood ran from puncture wounds in my knees. Skin I'd pampered for years was now marred with embedded pebbles and a twig or two. What was a simple scrape a few minutes ago looked like a skinning now.

"Oh, holy shit, that hurts." Injuries are a funny thing. When out of sight, they're often out of mind, but once seen—a hundred times felt.

"Welcome to the ranch, Natalie." He looked at me like it was inventory day. "Although those heels make your legs look great, I'd recommend investing in a pair of boots." His arm wrapped around my waist in a firm grip while I limped to where he led me.

"You think my legs look nice?" *When did my voice get so sweet and soft?*

"Your legs look great, but they won't for long if you're not smart." With a click and a clunk, the tailgate of a silver pickup truck fell open, and the stud lifted me onto it. He inspected my injuries, but his eyes strayed to the extra bit of thigh I was showing. I should have pulled the fabric closed, but I liked the way his eyes lingered on my skin. "Stay here."

Like I was going anywhere. My neck stretched to watch him walk away. Long legs covered in denim strode with confidence toward the passenger side of the truck. The blue fabric hugged his thighs like a jealous lover—gripping and pulling. Heat coursed through me, despite the sun sitting low on the horizon. I sucked in a cooling breath. I needed some of that.

Mr. Tall, Blond, and Delectable returned with a black satchel and dumped its contents next to me. "You a doctor?" *Lord, the ranch is looking better all the time!*

"I am, but generally speaking, my patients aren't quite as lovely as you. Lately, it's been all asses to elbows."

He grabbed a bottle of water and poured it over my cuts, dabbing the injury with a piece of wadded-up gauze. I flinched each time he came in contact with my abraded skin, but I warmed each time his thumb brushed above the wound. A touch meant to comfort, but it managed to heat me to the core. I felt its impact more than the wound.

"Gynecologist?" My voice cracked. "Proctologist?" A physician at the ranch? That was some kind of medical plan she provided. House calls and all. I was furiously trying to come up with an ailment that would keep this man coming back to "doctor" me.

With a pair of tweezers, he picked out the remaining debris and gently covered the area with a large Band-Aid. "I'm a vet. My name is Roland."

The man doctoring me spent his days sticking thermometers up animals' asses. *If he's a vet and I'm the patient, what kind of animal does that make me?*

"You're Roland? No way!" I slapped my hand over my mouth to stop anything else from coming out.

"Yes." He dipped a clean piece of gauze into the water and dabbed at whatever blood I'd transferred to my face. "Way." Again, he mocked me.

I shook my head and opened my mouth, but not a thing came out. This man was the nice guy? He was the brother figure?

"No fucking way." The words could not be contained. Nor could my shock. "Are you even qualified to help me?"

"This isn't neurosurgery, sweetheart; it's a Band-Aid." He finished with my hands and lifted me off the truck and back onto my way-too-tall shoes. Hands on my shoulders, he turned me toward the cabins and pointed to the one on the end. "That's yours. Be careful on your way over there. I'd hate for you to fall on your pretty face. I'm fresh out of bandages."

"You think my face is pretty?" A day at the spa, and I'd be passable, but to call me pretty right now was an overstatement.

"Yes, until you open your dirty little mouth."

Chapter 3

NATALIE

A shiver of excitement ran through my body and tingled in all the places that hadn't been touched by a man in years. Roland might have fooled everyone else, but not me. That man wasn't a nice guy. He was a bad boy in disguise. The way his free hand brushed up my thigh to the split in my skirt—that was bad in such a good way. I looked over my shoulder, but he was gone, so I continued on my way.

Uneven steps brought me to the first cabin in a row of eight. The minute I hit the front porch, I kicked off the black pumps that pinched my toes and rubbed my heels raw. These had once been my comfortable everyday shoes. Now they felt like a tool of torture, something akin to foot binding. I'd never thought I'd say it, but I already missed the baggy prison uniforms and the slip-on canvas shoes. They did nothing for my figure, but they didn't chafe my body parts either.

Where was everyone? A quick glance around, and I was certain I was alone. There weren't any cars parked by the cabins, and the only movement seen or heard nearby was the clip-clop of horse hooves and distant murmur of men—probably the ranch hands—or maybe Roland.

Set Up

How was I supposed to approach my house? Did I knock at my door, hoping the girls were tucked up inside waiting for me? Was I supposed to sit on the porch swing and wait for Mickey to appear from who knows where? Instead of standing on the porch and debating, I acted. I slid my fingers over the brass knob and turned.

Don't wait for permission; beg for forgiveness was my family's motto.

Tension rose with each second. What did a ranch cabin look like inside? Would I be forced to sleep on the bottom bunk in my room? I closed my eyes and pictured the worst possible scenario.

I conjured up a vision of an old wooden rocker, straight out of a 50s Western, placed in front of a stone fireplace. A metal bar teetered on a frame as the cast-iron pot, bubbling with buffalo chili, swung back and forth. Its contents seeped over the blackened finish and hissed upon hitting the dying embers. Above the mantel hung the head of the beast now dead and heating in the pot. Its eyes pinned me with accusation.

Traveling around the space in my imagination, I entered the bedroom, where a pallet covered with hay sat in the corner. Four hooks lined the wall. No closet. No dresser. Just enough hooks to hold my winter coat, my Sunday dress, my pajamas, and my bib overalls.

The bathroom across from the bedroom was enough for me. Once I saw the hole in the floor, I snapped my eyes wide and threw open the door. Reality had to be better than the nightmare I imagined.

Relief washed over me. Front and center was the living room, decorated with simple but tasteful furnishing. Cream-colored chairs flanked a darker sofa. Hardwood tables sat strategically placed so every seat had a resting spot for a drink or maybe a TV dinner. Lord knows I'd be eating a lot of those. I didn't have the first clue about cooking. The last food preparation method I'd Googled was how to hard boil an egg. I tried it, and if the name "hard boiled" meant the whites and the yolks were supposed to be hard, I'd failed miserably. Unless they were called "hard boiled" because they were hard to boil; in that case, I'd done OK.

My idea of cooking was to show up to The Eatery, a gourmet

food store, and purchase something pre-made. Once you slapped it on a piece of china, no one knew you hadn't slaved away at the stove all day preparing it.

Barefoot, I entered the living room. The plush tan carpet cushioned my sore feet, its pile pushing between my toes like sand at the beach. Heaven.

For three years, I'd been walking on stained concrete. The only relief from the cold stone was the moment I undressed and stood on my dirty clothes.

"What do you think?"

I jumped several inches into the air and landed softly back onto the lush carpet. "Shit, Mick, you scared me!"

"Sorry. I did tap on the front door, but you didn't budge. Lost in thought? Where were you?"

"Is it possible to orgasm in your toes?" I pushed my feet into the soft fibers and shimmied back and forth. "This is amazing. Thank you." Two steps forward, and I was wrapped around her like a pretzel.

"It's a good thing you came here straight from prison; otherwise, you'd be in a different kind of shock. It's not what you're used to, but it's clean and comfortable."

"You're right, it's not what I'm used to. I'm going to miss the bunks and Lacey Taylor's snoring. Then there's Terry Schooner's flatulence problem." I glanced around the space again. The cabin was all right. "Then there's the community bathroom. How will I live without creepy Karen eye-fucking me every day in the bay?"

Mickey walked into the kitchen, where I followed. Silver appliances that would never be used shone under the recessed lighting. She opened the fridge to show me it was stocked and pulled two wine coolers from the top shelf. "Karen was jealous of what Debra had." Mickey popped the tops and walked to the living room, where she plopped into one of the side chairs. She leaned back and lifted her boots to the coffee table. I took a seat on the couch where the deep cushions wrapped around my bottom and hugged me.

"What did Debra have?" I was playing stupid. I knew she was

referring to the overstated rumor that I'd let Debra Watson go down on me.

"A safe place between your thighs?"

I took a long draw from the bottle and relished the bubbles as they tickled and slid down my throat. "Let's clear this up. I did get some action, but not as much as everyone says. In fact, I can count those times on one hand." I peeled back the sweaty wrapper and thought about those moments that had both shamed and satisfied me. "The thing is, I never had sex with Debra. Not in my mind anyway. When my eyes were closed, those moments were shared with whomever I chose. I had several conjugal visits with Ryan Gosling. That's my story, and I'm sticking to it."

Mickey lifted her bottle into the air. "Here's to your freedom, your future, and sex with Ryan Gosling."

Just then, the door burst open and Holly and Megan ran in with their arms full of bags. They dropped them next to the couch and smothered me with hugs.

It was so nice to be with friends again. I felt bad for Robyn. She was the lone ranger left behind, but not for long. She'd be here in a few months.

The girls sat on each side of me, squeezing me between them like the creamy sweet filling between two yummy cookies. Holly sat to my left, her baby bump just beginning to show. Megan to my right was sporting a Grand Canyon smile.

"Are you bragging about your nights with Ryan Gosling again?" Holly rested her hands on her blooming stomach.

"Oh my God, listen to me." I could feel the heat of embarrassment rise to my cheeks. "I'm not into girls. I'm into orgasms, and when you close your eyes, you can't tell whose tongue it is, so let it be." I pulled the drink to my lips and gulped it down. I was hot, thirsty, and mortified that the girls would tell everyone. "Don't be spreading rumors about me. I need to get laid, and most men's egos couldn't handle that story."

Megan rolled forward and stood. "Can I get a drink from your refrigerator?"

"Oh," I groaned. "What a crap hostess I am. I'm out of practice. Let me get you something."

I rocked back and forth, trying to get the momentum to stand. With a sofa that curled around me like a hammock, I was likely to spend my life planted right here. It felt that good.

Megan placed a single finger on my shoulder and pushed me back into the fluffy confines. "Nope, I got it." She looked at Holly. "Juice for you?"

Pride and sunshine radiated from Holly's smile. "How about water?"

"Sure thing," Megan said.

Mickey finished off her wine cooler and stood. "I wish I could stay, but we have the youth rodeo in a couple of weeks, and there's so much to do." She leaned over me and kissed me on the forehead. "Meet us outside a few minutes to six, and I'll drive you to Rick's." She looked down at my bandaged knees. "Looks like Roland doctored you up."

I thought about the sexy blond with eyes a shade darker than Tiffany blue and felt a thrill coarse through my body. "Yes, he cleaned the dirty from me and slapped on a few Band-Aids."

The girls all laughed, then Mickey added, "They say you can take the girl out of the trailer park, but you can't take the trailer park out of the girl. I'm sure the same could be said for dirt. Roland is skilled, but I don't think he has what it takes to get all the dirty out of you, girlfriend." She turned on her heels and walked out.

Hell yeah, Roland could try to take the dirty out of me. I'd be game for a more thorough examination and cleanup job.

Megan handed a bottle of water to Holly and took Mickey's chair.

I raised my hands in the air and shouted, "What's up, bitches?"

The girls spilled their news for nearly an hour before they noticed the time was getting away from them.

"Oh hell," Holly said. "We have to get ready for Rick's."

Megan looked at the pile of packages left by the couch. "Sorry, we weren't here when you showed up. We were out getting you some essentials, like body wash, lotion, and make-up."

Set Up

I sat up straight. "Make-up?" If happiness could be defined by a word, 'make-up' would be it—or maybe it would come second, right after men. Or maybe third, with men and money coming in one and two. Oh hell, it would be in the top ten. There were other things to consider, like chocolate, bubble baths, pedicures, and designer labels.

Holly scooted to the edge of the cushion and pulled items from the bag. "We didn't know what to get exactly, so we bought a bunch of stuff. You can take back what you don't use. It's standard stuff, like mascara and lipstick, blush, and eyeshadow." She set the items out on the coffee table one by one. "Not the brands you're used to, but a temporary substitution. We also picked you up a few more items, like a decent bra and something other than granny panties." She reached for the pink Victoria's Secret bag and drew out a pink lacy bra with matching underwear.

"Oh, holy hell." I stole the garments from Holly's hands and jumped up from the couch. Hellfire spread across my bandaged knees while I danced around the room, but I didn't care. In my hands sat women's gold. I ran my fingers over the lace. It wasn't as fine as La Perla or made from silk, like Myla, but it was all girl, and I was ecstatic. "I'm speechless. I'm excited. I might even get laid tonight."

"Not wearing that." Megan pointed at my skirt and blouse.

"Besides being terribly out of fashion and torn, what's wrong with this?"

I pulled at the hem of the skirt. Though too tight, it wasn't too short or too long. It was a pleasant gray and made out of the finest wool. Matched with the soft pink shirt and black heels, it served its purpose.

"It's fine if you want to drop to your knees in front of the CEO of a law firm, but you're in cowboy country."

One look at my bandaged knees, and I knew I wouldn't be dropping to them anytime soon. Equally unappealing was the thought of dressing like the other girls.

Holly wore a sundress and cowboy boots. Her look came straight out of Beauty and Boots catalogue—a company I knew well from my previous life when I worked for the firm that did their accounting. Each time they emailed their records, they attached a copy of their advertisements. Megan, on the other hand, was in a T-shirt and jeans with the obligatory pair of boots thrown in.

"I'm supposed to dress like you two?"

The girls laughed. "No," Megan said. "We can pull this off and look fabulous. You'll have to try harder." She pulled a phone from her pocket and looked at the screen. "We gotta go."

Holly plopped the rest of the bags on the table and stood. "There are a bunch of clothes in your closet. Probably not your thing, but they'll keep you covered until you can get something better." Her sad eyes connected with mine. Then she hugged me and whispered, "I'm sorry your mom wasn't there. I know what that feels like."

Poor Holly had lost her mom while she was in jail. But by the way she described her, only death would have kept them apart. My mother was alive, on the other hand, and she was absent.

"Shake a leg, girlfriend," Megan said. "You have forty-five minutes, and then it's party time." Arm in arm, two of my favorite people walked out the door.

I ran my hand through dry brittle hair and sighed. I needed forty-five minutes for a good conditioning, and another hour to rinse the prison stench from my body.

"Chop-chop—get a move on," I told myself.

Chapter 4

NATALIE

Dressed in hand-me-down blue jeans, a cotton tank, and a plaid shirt I tied around my waist, I walked out of the cabin intent on embracing everything, even the worn cowboy boots that completed my straight-off-the-farm look. If there was one thing I was good at, it was fitting in.

Crisp and cool with a scent of hay and horses, a breeze floated between the cabins, picked up my hair, and added a trace of citrus to the mix. A hum of voices acted like a GPS, leading me to cabin seven, where Holly stood with a man who could have modeled for a living. On his knees, he pressed his lips to her stomach, and I melted. Without a doubt, he was Keagan, Holly's husband.

"You'll have to share your training routine. I've always wanted to know how to drop a man to his knees."

The big cowboy rolled back on his boots. "You must be Natalie." He stood as tall as a pine tree with thick, strong limbs. "Welcome home." I could understand how Holly had fallen so hard for the man. His smile alone could warm an iceberg.

"Thanks."

Home was such a strange word, considering the variety of places it had encompassed for me in the past several years. It had meant the mansion in Cherry Creek, the dorm room at college, the meager apartment in Denver, and lastly the prison. Now I was a resident of Second Chance Ranch, which was less like a halfway house for ex-cons and more like a dude ranch without a spa.

"Are you getting settled in?" he asked.

"It was odd to take a shower without shoes, to walk barefoot across the carpet, and to reach into a refrigerator because I could, but I'm liking it all."

"A shower without shoes was my favorite post-prison experience, and the Keurig…holy smokes, it's like having a Starbucks in your kitchen," Holly said.

"And I thought I was the best part of your post-prison experience." Keagan leaned in and whispered something into Holly's ear. "You liked that, right?"

Her cheeks blossomed cherry red. "You know it." Obviously, they were sharing an intimate moment.

"Just checking." He leaned in and gave her a sweet kiss on the lips. "You two ready?"

"Are you two trying to kill me?" I pointed to my chest. "Single and reluctantly celibate here, and your little show of affection is making me swoon."

Holly pulled an arm through mine. Like she was going to tell me a secret, she tilted her head and, with a voice loud enough to be heard in the stable, said, "Honey, there's nothing little about Keagan."

"Oh, my God." I rolled my eyes to heaven. "Rub it in." I looked over my shoulder toward Keagan, who somehow stood taller and broader after his wife's words.

Quick and agile, he raced around to open the door to a big black truck. As if she weighed nothing, he picked Holly up and put her into the front seat. For me, he offered his hand as a boost into the back seat.

"I thought I was driving with Mickey."

Click

Click

Click

Keagan was in the driver's seat, and we were buckled up and ready to go.

"Mickey's tied up on a phone call about the Junior Rodeo," Keagan explained. "Who knew how much work one of these events would require? The paperwork alone would send me to an early grave."

"Will it bring a good return on investment to the ranch?" That was the accountant in me speaking. She'd been silenced for so long.

"No, it's all volunteer and charity. The local 4-H and Peak Animal Rescue are the recipients of all the proceeds." Keagan tugged on Holly's belt one more time before he started the truck and drove away.

I leaned forward, resting my chin on the leather seat in front of me. "The ranch has to get something from it. I've been involved in a lot of charity events, and there's no use doing them if you're not getting something."

"I helped set it up," Holly said. "Working for Finishing Touches has helped me see that sometimes doing the right thing is reason enough."

I shivered at the thought of working in hospice. "You're a saint. I'm not sure I could work with people, knowing they're going to die soon."

"It's all about perspective," Keagan said. "You're with us right now, and someday we're going to die." He reached over and threaded his fingers through Holly's.

She smiled and nodded. "It's what you do with your living days that matters," she finished for him.

Jealousy had never been a bug that bit me, but it buzzed around me now. I'd known Holly for years, and she'd never seemed this happy before. The look of peace and tranquility suited her. She'd always been a sweetheart, but damn she looked good with that halo floating around her head.

"What to do with my days—*that* is the question. With a record, I don't imagine it will be easy to find a job."

Keagan and Holly shook their heads back and forth in unison. Did they realize they shared a brain and body? "You'll figure it out."

Holly reached her free hand over the seat back and gave mine a motherly pat. "Are you going to try to see your mom?"

"I have to. She's the master juggler, and my inheritance is one of the balls she keeps in the air."

My lineage was common knowledge. Being a trust fund baby wasn't a secret I could hide. What hadn't been divulged was the amount of money on the line. If I could get my mother to release my inheritance, I'd be set for life. As the executor, she controlled everything, which made it imperative to seek her out.

"I can't imagine what you feel like."

"Sure you can. Take your pain and cut it into quarters. Then give me twenty-five percent. My mother isn't dead. She's absent. Her not coming to see me isn't what pains me. I'm used to my mother pretending I don't exist. What hurts is not existing."

The tears that gathered in my eyes surprised me. I'd never been an emotional person. "Anyway, back to the ranch." I opened the window and let the air dry my unshed tears. "Goodwill and public opinion will go a long way to gain favor, so it would seem Mickey will be getting a boon after all."

"Since you have some experience with these things, maybe you can help?" Holly's voice lifted in question.

"Maybe." My immediate plans included a visit to see Mommy Dearest and a lot of sleeping in. Those five o'clock wake-ups were murder on a girl.

The sun was setting, and an orange glow burned from the horizon. A red tin roof in the distance looked like a flame licking the darkening sky.

"Tell me about Roland."

Controlled, I tried to remove all interest and excitement from my voice. *Never let your left hand know what your right hand is doing*, Grandma had told me. She was a strong believer in keeping people guessing, and I didn't need Holly to know I found the vet sexy. *Keep them on their toes, Natalie.* Her words of wisdom echoed in my head long after she died. *Take what's yours and run with it.* Well, I tried that one, and it landed me in prison for grand larceny.

"He's the sweetest man—next to my husband, of course." She

stroked her husband's ego like a happy-ending massage. "You have to love a guy who rescues animals, and I haven't seen an animal that doesn't love him. They're good judges of character and can pick out the good from the bad at a glance."

"I wouldn't know. Never had an animal, unless a Furby counts, and in all honesty, mine perished from lack of attention, or maybe the batteries died. I'm not sure."

Keagan and Holly were laughing when we pulled into the parking lot of the building with the fiery red roof.

"Look there." Holly pointed toward a silver truck. "Roland beat us all."

Tha thump

Tha thump

Tha thump, tha thump, tha thump

Roland was here waiting for us…for me. Or maybe it was like Mickey said—it was required, and the incentive was free food and beer. Either way, I'd get another chance to meet the man who made my heartbeat quicken and thighs quiver.

"By the way," Holly said, "you look amazing. It's as if you've been living on the ranch all your life."

She brushed my hair off my shoulder. It was such a mom thing to do. I looked down at the swell of her belly and thought, *What a damn lucky kid to be living there.*

"Just trying to blend in," I replied. 'Chameleon' was how Officer Ellis described me, but I'd always likened myself to a fairy. A little sprinkle of dust, and I could become anything.

"Ready?"

The door opened, and Keagan helped me to the ground. His truck was a hell of a lot easier to slide out of than Mickey's, but that could also have been the absence of the black stilettos.

"I need alcohol, wings, and a man."

Keagan stepped between Holly and me. "I can get you the alcohol and wings, but you're on your own when it comes to men."

Chapter 5

ROLAND

It was early and a Thursday night, but there was always one woman who felt the rhythm of the jukebox, no matter what. Tonight, she danced for an audience of four like she was on stage at the Fine Arts Center. Eyes closed, she swayed to the beat like it was a mating dance. And to many it was, but I was over that shit. At thirty-two, I'd watched my share of dancers, bought a lot of drinks, and witnessed too many walks of shame. It never worked out for me. I was the nice guy, and nice guys always finished last.

Money was exchanged between two ranch hands. No doubt a bet on who was taking her home. A fool's bet. She'd never leave with anyone. She'd dance until the drinks stopped coming. Then she'd hop in a cab alone. I knew her game. In fact, I'd played her game, and she'd cost me a pretty penny in pink frozen concoctions.

"Two pitchers of light beer, one Sprite, and a dozen tequila shots."

Rick didn't blink an eye at the order. He was used to crews coming in on any given night to let off a bit of steam. As part of M and M Ranch, I was no stranger here.

"Same table in the back?" Rick nodded to the corner where we gathered on a regular basis.

Set Up

"Yep. We got another one."

It was no secret Mickey had started a halfway house for ex-cons. The joke was, she brought all the pretty girls home to marry her staff. It was one way to keep good men on the ranch. Put a beautiful, willing woman there, and he'd never go anywhere.

I'd been through all of them. Not in the sense of dating and bedding them, but I'd had a chance with every one of them, and they all played the nice guy card with me. I was done being a nice guy.

"Is this one a looker?"

Rick eased the pitcher from under the tap and shoved the second one in its place. He smoothed his bushy gray mustache and ran his free hand through the six hairs left on his head.

"She's finer than frog hair split seven ways."

The door swung open and washed the dark bar in a sea of light. It was right out of the movies, where out of the light emerged an angel.

Well, now, isn't that a sight.

On the heels of Keagan and Holly was Natalie. All five feet and some of her. I skimmed my eyes from the top of her chestnut hair to the black cowboy boots on her feet. She walked with confidence and a slight limp toward the back table.

"Oh, holy hell," Rick said. "That one's trouble."

"How do you know?"

"It's written all over her, man. Look at that smile. Look at that rack. Look at that ass."

Rick plopped the second pitcher on the tray, sending a splash of suds over the edge. Lining up twelve shot glasses, he kept his eye on the girl while he upturned the bottle and ran a line of liquor down the row.

"She's bad for your business."

"Don't I know it. But she is a sight to see." He stared at Natalie. His eyes sparkled with appreciation.

"No, I mean she's bad for your business." I gripped the bottle and turned it upright. Rick had been moving the bottle down the row but missed most of the glasses. Twelve near empty glasses sat in a puddle at the bar.

"Ah, hell."

I chuckled and picked up the tray of beer and mugs. "I'll be back for those shots. And don't forget a Sprite for Holly."

Rick was busy wiping up the day's profits when I left the counter.

Keagan met me halfway. "This one's yours," he said only to me.

I shook my head hard enough to give myself whiplash. "Nope. I'm over it."

"Says this head." He cuffed my ear. "Start thinking with the other for a change."

With my hands full, I couldn't retaliate, and he knew it. *Coward.* Over his shoulder, I saw Natalie taking in the place and wondered whether she was shopping the near-empty market. With just a handful of men present, her pickings were slim. She looked at me and smiled—a damn movie star smile—teeth lined up like straight pickets from a whitewashed fence.

Not falling for a damn smile. Instead, I nodded and placed the tray down.

"Evening, Natalie." I nodded toward the others. "Holly. Keagan." Then I turned to Keagan and walloped him on the side of the head. "Respect your elders, asshole."

The girls' mouths were left hanging open while I turned and walked away. Behind me, I heard Holly ask, "Did you deserve that?"

"Damn straight," Keagan yelled at the end of a hearty laugh.

By the time I returned with the Sprite, shots, lime slices, and salt, the rest of the gang was there. Crammed into the booth were Tyson, Cole, Killian, and Megan. On the end was Natalie. Sitting in bar stools pulled up to the table were Keagan, Holly, Mickey, and Kerrick.

Kerrick took the tray from my hands and nodded toward the only empty seat—the one next to Natalie. No accident there. Shots were placed in front of everyone but Holly.

"Here's to Robyn, who will be here soon, and to Natalie," Mickey said in a toast. "May her heart and her snatch stay full."

Set Up

Natalie let out a screech that could break glass. "You did not just say that in front of everyone!" No one was paying attention to her indignation but me. They were tossing back the tequila and laughing.

I felt sorry for her. Unlike the other strays Mickey brought home, Natalie wasn't ranch material. If I were a betting man, I'd say she was country club, born and raised. There was something about money that oozed from the skin of people with it. Natalie had an air about her that screamed wealth. Not even a few years in the slammer could take that away.

I slid into the booth next to her. Everything from our shoulders to our thighs touched, and I liked it more than I wanted. "Ignore them. They hang out with animals all day. It's rubbed off on them."

"What's your excuse?"

"I wasn't talking about your snatch."

She blushed. "No, but earlier you told me I had a dirty little mouth." She licked her lips.

The simple act made my cock twitch. I liked her dirty little mouth, but that was something I'd keep to myself. I pushed the shot toward her and held up her hand. "Lick it." Her tongue ran slowly over the space between her finger and thumb. I salted it and picked up a lime. "Bottoms up."

She licked the salt, tossed back the tequila, and waited for me to give her the lime. When I placed it on her lips, she pulled it and my finger into her mouth. The velvety caress sent my dick into overdrive. It had been way too long since I'd been laid.

When she was finished, the table was silent. The single guys were dumbstruck, their eyes filled with lust. The couples were smiling like they had a secret. But I had news for them. No way, no how was I hooking up with Natalie. She was wrong for me. I leaned in and inhaled her citrus scent. All wrong. I was hay, and she was orange blossom. I was blue jeans, and she was tight skirts. I was boots, and she was sexy, impractical heels. Except for tonight— tonight she was perfect, and perfect looked too damn good on her to be good for me. Those jeans fit her ass like a wet leather glove. And those boots would look amazing propped on my shoulders while my face was buried between her legs.

Mickey and Kerrick interrupted my thoughts. "Wings and fries okay for everyone?"

After nods from around the table, they rose and headed toward Rick at the bar. The single men took a lingering last look at Natalie before they went to try their luck with the girl on the dance floor. Keagan and Killian chatted about the pregnant mares while Holly and Megan talked about baby stuff. That left me and Natalie on our own.

"Thanks for helping me out today."

"No problem. It's what I do."

"I heard you were the nice guy."

"Grrrr." That statement irked me. "Don't believe everything you hear."

She chewed her lip, turning it plump and red. "There's nothing wrong with a nice guy."

"Sweetheart, I'm not as nice as they'd have you believe."

She tilted her head and bit harder on her lip.

I plucked at her bottom lip with my thumb. "There's no Band-Aid for that lip of yours if you bite it through."

Natalie let her swollen lower lip pop free. Yes, this woman definitely had game. All that lip biting and cooing were part of the setup. I'd give her about ten minutes to prove me right. She'd come on to me, and that would be it. I could take her up on it and be done with it once and for all, or I could ignore her come-on and save myself the hassle. One scenario took care of my hard dick; the other, my conscience. I could deny being the nice guy, but that's what I was. My parents raised me to love and revere women, not use and discard them.

I thought with the head on my shoulders. It was completely against the bro code, but I wasn't interested in one-night stands. I'd had plenty of those, and I wanted something more. I wanted long-term. I wanted a wife and kids. All Natalie wanted was a stiff dick, and I was pretty sure she wasn't going to be particular.

She eyed the remaining shots on the table. "Can I have another?" Her sweet voice caressed my skin like a velvet glove.

"Knock yourself out." I swept the three remaining shots toward her.

"I'll pass on the knocking-out part. Almost did that today getting out of the truck." She skipped the salt and lime, going straight for the shot.

"Drink too many of those, and you'll have the same problem." I flagged down the cocktail waitress who had recently shown up for her shift and asked for a round of waters.

"I've got about ninety-nine problems, and falling on my face is the only one that can't be solved with a lot of tequila."

Was this where I was supposed to ask her about her problems? Not happening. I knew her problems. She was an ex-con who hadn't been laid in years. She had no money and nowhere else to go.

"Do you want to go crib shopping with us tomorrow?" Holly asked.

It was funny to watch Natalie's face contort. She looked like she'd rather amputate a limb than baby shop with the girls.

She popped back the third shot and shivered. "Sorry," she said in that way girls do without meaning it. "I've got to visit Mommy Dearest and persuade her to loosen the purse strings."

Holly and Megan exchanged looks with Natalie.

"Should we get you another shot?" Holly asked.

"Nope, I'm good. Roland here has been taking very good care of me." She gripped my arm and leaned her head against my shoulder. "I like you, Roland." Her words had taken on a slow, sexy drawl. "I wasn't convinced earlier, but you *are* a nice guy." She rubbed her breasts into my arm. "Later, we can be nice to each other."

"And then what?" I knew the drill. A roll in the sheets, and then she'd pretend I didn't exist. That wouldn't work. I spent a lot of time at the ranch, and I didn't want a reason to feel uncomfortable there.

"We can figure it out."

Not willing to succumb to her charm and find myself sneaking out of her cabin in the early morning hours, I pried her off my arm. "I like you, too, Natalie, but I'm not looking for a project or an STD." My words were uncharacteristically cruel.

I stood up, and all eyes at the table were on me. Holly and Megan pierced me with evil glares while the men looked on with confusion.

"I've got to go. I've got clinic hours tomorrow."

When I turned and walked away, Natalie's voice followed. "What in the hell is wrong with him?"

I had to ask myself the same question.

Chapter 6

NATALIE

Ka-bang
  Ka-bang
Ka-bang

When I woke, I wasn't sure whether the banging was real or in my head. After Roland left, I went straight for the beer. The saying "beer after liquor, never been sicker" had a ring of truth to it. I wasn't going to throw up, but my head was screaming all kinds of expletives at me. Roland thought I had a dirty mouth before—if only he could've heard what I had to say to him now. Words like "jackass" and "asshole" were on the cleaner side of things I wanted to spew at him.

I tossed back the covers of the most comfortable bed I'd slept on in years and trudged to the bathroom. I flipped the light switch and looked in the mirror.

Oh hell, I thought sourly, *it's not like I don't have enough baggage to deal with today, and now there are two steamer trunks sitting under my eyes.*

Cold water and coffee were part of my immediate plan. Dressed in yesterday's clothes, I practically fell out the front door in search of the incessant banging coming from the back of the cabin. I stumbled down the stairs with a mug of coffee in one hand and my aching head pressed to the other.

Ka-bang
Ka-bang
Ka-bang

I found the culprit out back. Toby was making his way from post to post, nailing in the boards that had come loose.

"Stop." I set my coffee on the top of the post and pressed my hands to my pounding head. "My head is going to explode. Must you start so early?" The young man tipped his head back and smiled.

"We start when the sun rises and end when it sets." He lifted the hammer to strike again.

"Please," I begged. "Can't you start the noisy stuff later?"

"This is a working ranch, darlin'. Besides, it's after nine. By ranch standards, it's almost time for lunch."

I didn't know what shocked me more: the fact that I couldn't convince him to stop, or that it was after nine. Just before Mickey had poured me into bed, she'd told me she'd give me a ride to my mom's at ten. That meant I had less than an hour to pull myself together.

With my half-full mug of coffee back in my hand, I took off like a race horse toward my door.

Toby's voice followed me to the door. "Take two painkillers and drink lots of water."

Once inside, I switched into high gear. Showered and feeling partially human, I rummaged through the hand-me-downs in the closet. One outfit hit the floor, followed by the next and the next until all of the clothes I had were piled high at the end of the bed.

None of this would do. One look at me, and my mother would mistake me for a vagrant trying to break in. Shuffling through the pile, I chose the clothes she would find least offensive. The best I could come up with was black jeans and a light pink tunic.

At five minutes to ten, I exited the cabin and waited on the porch swing. Back and forth I rocked. It was a comfortable motion. A reminder of the dance Mother and I did. She'd push, and I'd relent. I'd push, and she'd give in. Who would be pushing today?

A cloud of dust beat the old blue truck to the cabin. Mickey rolled down the window. "You ready?"

"As ready as I can be." I slid out of the swing. My strides were short and slow. I walked like a prisoner on the green mile.

"How's the head?" She put the truck in gear and tore out of the gravel parking lot like a cat with a dog on its tail.

Two fingers on each temple helped soothe the ache that came from stupidity, but the ache that came from Roland's words hurt more. They shouldn't have. Who was he to me? No one. But to insinuate I carried a communicable disease was wrong.

"I'll survive." I took my hands off my head to pick at the scab forming on my palm from yesterday's fall. "You said Roland was the nice guy. Why was he mean to me?"

Mickey's head bobbled. "I have no idea. What did you do to him?"

Without thinking about my aching head, I shifted around to look at her. The movement sent sharp daggers of unpleasantness slicing through my brain.

"Me?" I pulled on the seatbelt, trying to get more room. "All I did was tell him I liked him, and he went after me like a rabid dog."

"That's not like him. Are you sure you didn't do something?"

"So it's my fault." After a shake of my head, I growled. "Fine, I'm to blame. Story of my life. The thing is, Mick, I didn't expect it to come from you, too."

"If you're going to survive in this life, Natalie, stop playing the part of the victim. I know it's a role you've perfected, but you need to change the script."

I had nothing to say to that. We drove the rest of the way in silence, broken only by my terse instructions at each turn until she pulled into my old Cherry Creek neighborhood. Not the tiny apartment I'd lived in before I went to prison, but the mansion my mother owned.

"Shit..." Her mouth opened so wide, her chin almost hit her chest. "You said your family had money, but—"

"They do."

"No kidding, but I was thinking doctor rich, not Oprah rich."

Mickey slowed to a crawl and drove up the street like she was casing the neighborhood. Her truck looked out of place among the high-end SUVs and sports cars that hugged the curbs. *How long would it take one of Mom's friends to call the police to report a suspicious vehicle in the area?* Even the lawn care providers drove models from the current decade.

"We aren't the Rockefellers, but my family isn't in jeopardy of being homeless anytime soon." The sun visor creaked when I pulled it down. What greeted me in the tiny mirror horrified me. My skin was sallow; my hair hung like an old, dirty mop around my shoulders. Thank goodness I was limited to a glimpse. I couldn't handle the full view. "Third house on your right. The one with the wrought-iron gate."

She pulled in front of the driveway and killed the engine. "You want me to wait?"

Part of me screamed *yes*, but that was silly. Mickey had a ranch to run, and I needed to get into my mom's good graces. That meant a lot of ass kissing and compliments. "No, I've got this. I'll see you later." My voice projected a confidence I didn't feel.

"You have a way to get home?"

"See that garage?" I pointed to the six-car monstrosity that formed an entire wing of the house. "Last time I was here, it was full. I'm sure Mom can spare a car."

"If you say so, but a woman who can't spare a minute can't be counted on for a car." She turned the key, and the truck coughed, then died. Again and again, she cranked the engine over until it caught and revved to life. I wasn't the only one who needed a new ride.

"Natalie?"

I stood at the curb and leaned into the open window.

"Don't forget I love ya."

"Love ya, too." And I did. Mickey and the girls were the best thing that came out of prison.

I stood there until the blue beast rounded the corner and

Set Up

vanished, leaving only a thick plume of black smoke in its wake. I was on my own.

Out of practice, I needed to pull from every reserve of patience I had to face my mom. She'd expect remorse, an apology, and compliance, so I tried to get in touch with my penitent child, but she was nowhere to be found. She was probably still sitting on the steely steps of the prison, waiting to be picked up.

Instead, I rolled my shoulders back and walked forward. At the keypad, I pressed the old code, 0916, but it didn't open. I cleared the screen and tried again with the same results, so I rang the bell. What if no one answered? What if I were stranded here with nothing but an expired debit card and spare change?

"Hello?" The sweetest voice came from the little black box. Relief filled every cell of my body.

"Rosa?" My throat tightened.

"Yes."

"It's me, Natalie." This she already knew; there was a state-of-the-art surveillance system. No one came to the gate without being seen.

"Hold on, Natalie. I'll get your mother."

That didn't bode well for me. There was no rush of excitement. The gates didn't open. My heart took a tumble and clattered to the ground. *Maybe Mickey should have waited*, I thought uneasily. Just when I was ready to turn and walk away, the gate shifted. It opened with a creak to let me in, then it slammed shut with a crash, locking me inside.

Mom stood by the front door dressed to the nines—classic Chanel, to be precise. The black and white power suit was no accidental choice. She knew I'd show up, and she'd dressed to intimidate.

"Hurry up, Natalie. I don't have much time." Her heels clicked across the tile in a fierce staccato. For a moment, I was back in prison, listening to the officers' boots striking the cement floors in that endless round of making sure we were where we should be. "Are you coming?"

Did I have a choice? If I lagged or protested, she would badger

41

me until I caved. Far easier to shuffle along behind her, my actions and choices as narrow as they had been in the Denver Women's Correctional Facility.

The only thing my mother's house lacked was bars. In the years I'd been gone, nothing much had changed. Hard marble floors buffed to an institutional shine. Cold glass everywhere. The only hint of color and warmth came from a fresh, floral arrangement that sat on the stark entry table. Always hydrangeas, whether in season or not.

"I'm expected at the club. It's the ladies auxiliary luncheon."

"But Mom, can't we talk for a bit? There's so much to say." I followed her into the kitchen, where she pulled a set of keys from a hook on the wall.

"There's very little to say, Natalie."

"I disagree."

"You're very good at that. I thought three years in prison would teach you to be more agreeable."

Heat spread through my chest.

"You taught me to be disagreeable."

"Oh, Natalie, I haven't been perfect—no one is, but you can't blame disagreeable on me." She rushed around the house, picking up her jacket, her purse, and a folder left on the coffee table.

What had started as an ember inside of me turned into a spark. "What do you mean? I've been more than agreeable with you. I got a degree in finance when I wanted one in fashion. I did the pageants. I hosted your parties. I dated men you thought were acceptable. I worked at the firm."

"Yes, and that was my mistake. A mistake I set about rectifying when you stole your cousin's watch."

That little spark burst into a flame. "It wasn't hers!" I screamed while I gripped my hair and pulled. "Grandma promised that watch to me, and Aunt Josie gave it to Rachel. She gave what wasn't hers to give."

"And you stole what wasn't yours to take. The will was clear—the watch was to go to Rachel."

"Yes, it was." My tone was clipped and matter of fact. This

Set Up

wasn't a battle I would win, I realized, so it was time to change course. "The will is why I'm here. When will you release my inheritance?" I was supposed to get it at twenty-five, but Mom had petitioned to extend her executorship. She'd won.

She walked to the hallway mirror, where she pulled her lipstick from her purse. She slicked on the hot pink and pressed her lips together, then wiped at an invisible smudge under her eye.

"How old are you?"

"I'm your damn daughter. You know how old I am."

After a huff, Mom continued. "I'm completely aware of your age, but what I really want to know, Natalie, is when will you grow up?"

I spread my arms out and gave her a what-the-hell-are-you-talking-about look. "I'm grown up."

"Really?" She thumbed a smear at the corner of her lip. "Can you support yourself?"

"I could if you gave me what belongs to me." Mom grabbed her keys and walked toward the garage. "Where are you going?"

"I told you. I have a luncheon. People are depending on me. I'm not going to let them down."

"What about me? I'm depending on you." I ran after her into the garage.

"That's the problem, Natalie. You've depended on me for everything, and I've indulged you. Now it's time to depend on yourself."

"You're the worst mother ever!" I yelled, stopping her in her tracks.

She turned around and looked at me impassively. "Yes, I was. I coddled and spoiled you, but I think you're redeemable. How badly do you want that money?"

"Mom, I'm living in a cabin on a ranch, surrounded by horse shit and hay. I have spare change and hand-me-down clothes." I began to hyperventilate. "I have nothing."

"What happened to all those boyfriends? Where are your friends from college and work?" She pressed the key fob, and the Mercedes' lights blinked. "They're gone, Natalie, because you cared about yourself more than you cared about any of them. Make sure you don't do the same to whoever let you live on their ranch. Seeing you homeless would be worse than seeing you in jail. At least there I knew you were fed and housed."

"That's it? You're going to drive away?" My voice rose until I sounded like a wounded animal. "What do I have to do?"

Mom climbed into the car and started the engine. She rolled down her window. "Tell you what, I'll give you thirty days to make a difference in someone or something's life. Prove you're not the selfish, self-centered girl I raised."

I sucked in several breaths, trying to get a handle on the situation. "How am I supposed to do that?"

She shrugged. "I don't know, Natalie, adopt a dog or volunteer somewhere. Learn to love something or someone more than yourself."

Rosa showed up in the garage and handed me an envelope and a set of keys. "What's this?"

"It's all you have left, Natalie. Use it wisely." Mom pressed the garage door opener and drove away.

My tears fell freely. Rosa put the envelope and keys down and pulled me into her arms. My face flattened into the cushion of her breasts. I inhaled the scent of cinnamon and cloves—a scent I associated with love. I'd spent many moments here in her arms while she consoled me over trivial things like not getting Bon Jovi to sing at my sweet sixteen or when Tate Hollander called me a whore for going out with his best friend. We were just seventeen and barely dating—it wasn't like we'd been married!

"You're going to be okay," Rosa said soothingly. She had been with my family for as long as I could remember, and she was the one person here now, holding me. "Your mother loves you. This is harder on her than it will be on you."

"How can you say that?" I pushed back and rubbed the tears from my eyes—leaving streaks of mascara on the backs of my hands and no doubt on my face. "She has a mansion, a Mercedes, and an endless supply of money."

Rosa's eyes lost their light. "She has those things, but what are they without love? Your mother doesn't want you to turn out like her. She wants more for you."

I shook my head. "She wants me to have more by giving me less?"

"Yes, that's right. When you have less, Natalie, it helps you appreciate when you have more. Your mom wants you to find happiness in people, not things. How can you do that when you fill your voids with stuff?" Rosa picked up the envelope and keys. "Sometimes less is more, Natalie. I've packed the car with your belongings. Most of what you had was sold to pay for your legal fees. What's left is in the envelope."

I pressed the key fob and watched in horror as the ten-year-old beat up VW hatchback used by the help beeped. I looked around at the four remaining cars: three SUVs and a Corvette.

"She's giving me that piece of shit?"

Rosa's lips thinned with every shake of her head. "That piece of caca, as you call it, has served this family well for years." She turned and walked toward the house.

"What will you drive?"

Rosa turned and pointed to the Lexus. "Your loss is my gain." She smiled and walked into the house.

"Make sure to tell my mom I made a difference in your life," I called after her, only half-joking.

Rosa shook her head and closed me out.

Chapter 7

NATALIE

Left alone, I opened the car's doors and surveyed the bins in the hatchback. There was no way all the clothes I'd owned pre-prison fit in them. All my shoes, maybe, but even that was a stretch.

I swallowed the lump in my throat. I couldn't afford to shed more tears. Hell, I couldn't afford much of anything. My life had just been reduced to a bunch of blue bins, an envelope, and a hatchback, but I didn't have time to wallow. I had to find a way to make a difference in the life of someone or something. Mom had said to get a dog—if that's all it would take to get my inheritance, I was happy to get an ankle biter. Surely, I could return it when I got what I wanted.

Inside the glove compartment, I found the automatic door opener and a Cartier box. My breath quickened. The boom of blood rushing through me threatened to resurrect my headache. I knew without a doubt what I'd find inside. I flipped open the box and looked at Grandma's watch sitting on a bed of white satin. A small notecard was stuck to the top.

Was it worth it?
Rachel
Was it?

Set Up

In the end, if I ended up with the watch and my inheritance, yes, it was worth it. I pulled the watch free and placed it on my wrist, where it belonged. I snapped the box shut and opened the envelope. It contained legal documents like my birth certificate and passport, and proof of car insurance. At least that was something.

In the bottom was a stack of hundred dollar bills—a short stack. I counted them out twice and came up with fourteen. It wasn't enough to go shopping properly, but it was enough to get a pedicure, and I needed pampering.

Fifteen minutes later, I was sitting in my favorite salon, Maisy's, with my feet in a tub of bubbling, lavender-scented water, and a sparkling soda in my hand. This was my life. I had grown up with this, and she wanted to take it all away. I couldn't understand why my mother was being so cruel.

I sipped at the cool drink and analyzed my circumstances. I had no idea how to move forward. This whole situation was out of my lane. I had braced for battle, but inside I had hoped I'd show up and Mom would hug me. She'd be disappointed, but all I needed to do was smile, tell her I loved her, and she would say, "Let's go get a facial," or better yet, "Let's go shopping."

Instead, I had chased her around the house while she evaded me. No hug. No terms of endearment. Just an envelope and an ultimatum. My life was going places I wasn't prepared to navigate. I had $1,400, an ugly hatchback, and a Cartier watch. I lived in a cabin where sexy cowboys were a dime a dozen and the only one I liked couldn't stand me. What did it matter? If they kept nailing fence posts at nine in the morning, I might take that hammer to the side of one of their heads, and I'd be back in jail.

It wasn't until the nail technician began to rub my legs that I noticed my wet cheeks. When had the tears begun to flow again? Even my body was betraying me.

"Oh, honey, you okay?" Her English, although broken, was filled with genuine concern.

"I will be." I pulled my pant legs higher to avoid them getting wet, and in doing so I exposed my scraped-up knees. "I may have been reduced to coal, but I'll be a Diamond again soon."

The girl nodded her head, even though she didn't have a clue as to what I meant. "Who hurt you?" She pointed to the scab on my knee.

"Roland." I had no idea why I said it. She was talking about my knees, for which I was completely responsible. I was talking about my heart, which he'd flayed open with a careless statement.

"This man, he no good for you." She delivered the message like a circus fortuneteller. When I checked out, would she charge me more for the advice?

Roland probably wasn't good for me, but there was something intriguing about him. Despite his rock hard body, blond curls, and blue eyes, I was sure the attraction was something else. I'd never been turned down before, and I didn't like how that felt. I'd get a dog to make Mom feel better, and I'd get Roland to make me feel better.

By the time I left the spa, I was $100 poorer, but my toes were painted Passionate Pink and I had a plan. Money well spent.

In thirty days, I'd be on the list of the most eligible and rich bachelorettes. I'd have a hip flat in downtown Denver, and I'd have something most of the other rich singles didn't—a record.

Suck that, Rachel.

Thirty minutes later, I pulled in front of the cabin. Normal ranch sounds filled the air: lots of horses snickering, shouts of male voices, and that nonstop pounding of the hammer. If Toby insisted on banging something, I might consider sacrificing myself to stop the noise. Surely, not every single man on this ranch found me repulsive.

No cars were parked in front of Holly or Megan's cabin. They worked outside the ranch. Both of them had make-a-difference kind of jobs. Jobs that no doubt made them feel good but paid peanuts and turned their hair gray prematurely.

"How did it go?" Mickey's voice sent me into the air.

"Stop doing that." I pressed my hand to my chest to rein in my runaway heartbeat.

"Robyn would be disappointed. She taught you better."

"You're right, but I wasn't expecting to be caught off guard."

"Well, duh. 'Off guard' means when you least expect it." She looked past me to the white cube with wheels. "I bet that caught you off guard."

"It's not what I expected, for sure." My lips curled. "This was the housekeeper's car, but I'll make do for now."

"That's the spirit. You're doing well for a girl who expected to be driving a sports car. I'm proud of you."

"This is temporary. In a few weeks, I'll be driving anything I want." With one finger on my chin, I looked skyward. "Maybe I won't drive at all. I'll hire someone to take me wherever I choose to go. We can schedule a girls night out whenever we want, and I'll provide the designated driver."

"So you negotiated a way forward?" Mickey's face lit up. "That's awesome."

Refocusing on the car, I sighed. "Sort of. Mom wants me to prove I can make a difference in the world. How hard can that be?"

"Harder than you think. You want some help unloading the car?"

"See there, you're making a difference in my life." With a click of the fob, the hatchback popped open and several of the bins fell out. One opened and spilled its contents.

"Oh my God, she sent pictures. I can't wear pictures. I thought these were clothes and shoes. Important stuff. How am I supposed to move into the future if she insists on keeping me in the past? I already have a wardrobe three years out of date." I marched around the bin. "One of the bins that could have been filled with possibilities is filled with times I don't want to remember." When I was finished with my rant, I scooped the pictures from the ground and shoved them into the bin.

Mickey stood to the side with her arms across her chest. "Who the hell *are* you?"

Stunned by the power in her voice, I took a step back. "What do you mean?"

"I knew you were spoiled. I knew you were shallow. What I didn't know is how little you value the important stuff." Mickey flipped the lid off the box and pulled a picture from the top. "Who is this?"

I leaned in to take a peek. "My father."

She pulled another from the stack. "And this?"

"That's Malcolm, my high school boy toy. I was crazy about him."

She slapped the photos into the box and jammed the lid down. "Tell me those people are less important than a pair of Jimmy whatever shoes."

"Jimmy Choo shoes," I said in a tiny voice.

"Whatever. My point is you're materialistic and self-centered. I love you anyway, but not everyone will. You want to make it in this world, then you have to be better than you are because right now you're dust on the bottom of the bin of humanity. There are more important things than money and clothes. Look around you, Natalie. Open your damn eyes."

"Why are you being so mean to me?"

Mickey heaved in a breath. "Because I believe somewhere deep down inside of you is the real Natalie waiting to emerge. She's the girl who braided hair and made body scrub out of table salt and orange juice."

"That was nothing."

"Tell that to the women who for the first time in their lives felt worthy of something. Here was this rich girl giving of herself so they could somehow be on equal footing. Grow up, Natalie. Life is about more than what's in your bank account, and it's certainly about more than a pair of Jimmy whatever's."

"Choo," I whispered.

She heard me and let out a groan. "You want to make a difference? Help muck out a stall or two, or if that's below you, come to the office, and put those accounting skills to work. I'm knee-high in paperwork for this junior rodeo and could use a hand."

Mickey turned on her boots and stomped toward the stables, leaving me in blue bin hell.

Thirteen trips later, I sat on the couch with a sparkling water in my hand and a wall of bins in front of me. For the past twenty-four hours, all I had heard was what an awful person I was. In the recesses of my mind, I heard my father: *If it looks like a duck, swims like a duck, and quacks like a duck, then it probably is a duck.*

I cranked my neck left and right. *Pop, pop, pop.* The vertebrae cracked, and some of the tension faded.

Who are you? Mickey had asked me. Good question. I didn't have a damn clue. All my life, I'd been whoever I needed to be, but now I was confused. I'd tried on so many personalities, I could give Sybil a run for her money.

"Natalie, get your life together. Figure out who you are."

Those were Officer Ellis' final words of wisdom. Even he saw something lacking in me. All the while, I thought I was the shit. Now I was realizing I was shit.

Not ready to deal with the boxes, I did what any self-respecting girl would do: grab a wine cooler and turn on the television. Watching someone else's life implode on screen was therapeutic. When I finished watching *Forrest Gump*, I was motivated. If Tom Hanks' character could go from a simpleton to a rich man, I could certainly figure my life out. I had great legs, I was smart, and I'd have millions. I was ahead of the game.

And it *was* a game. That much I knew. Still dressed in black jeans and a pink tunic, I walked outside to take in the playing field.

Behind the cabins, Toby and Tyson worked with some horses. One ran in a circle tied to a rope. Its mane blew in the breeze. Funny how easy it was to perceive that horse as running free instead of tethered to a master.

I moved on toward the big stables and found Keagan talking to a fat horse.

"You want to meet her?"

I looked around me to be sure he wasn't speaking to someone else. "No." I shook my head. Animals didn't really take to me.

"Come here, Natalie." He had the kind of voice a girl didn't argue with. "This is Sahara. She'll be giving us a foal this summer."

No wonder the horse was as big as a barn. "Wow, you sure do like to hang around the babymamas, don't you?"

Keagan was tall on his own, but when pride took over, he

seemed to grow another foot. "I find purpose in bringing new life into the world. It makes me realize how insignificant I am in the scheme of things. Besides, I am the master breeder on this ranch." His look challenged me to discount his claim. Of course, I couldn't argue. Holly was living proof the guy had effective swimmers.

"Now you're bragging."

He showed me how to pet the mare and let me feed her a piece of an apple. She gave me a gift, too—a handful of slobber I wiped on Keagan's sleeve.

"Killian is in the arena training one of our troublemakers. You should go check it out."

Training troublemakers? Was that some kind of message? I made my way to the arena, hoping my journey wasn't leading me to an intervention. I already felt raw from Mickey's tongue-lashing.

What I found when I entered the arena was a monstrous black horse on its hind legs towering over Killian. The horse was terrifying, and yet Killian was in control. He was rock solid, not a flinch in him. If that were me, I would have been tucked behind something until the danger passed.

"Stay there," Killian called out.

I looked around and found no one else in the area. "No problem." There wasn't a chance in hell I'd enter that arena. Here on the sidelines was the perfect place to watch. Within minutes, Killian had the horse calm and walking the perimeter.

"How did you do that?" Somehow, I'd gone from pressing my back to the wall to hovering over the rail.

"I'm breaking old habits. She was allowed to behave badly for far too long, and now I'm giving her an adjustment. Nothing is beyond redemption." Killian tied the horse's lead to a center pole and walked toward me. "She's getting to know me. Animals are good judges of character. Each time we're together, I'm proving myself worthy of her respect."

"You really believe you can train that horse to be docile?"

Killian jumped over the fence and stood in front of me. "No. I believe I can teach her to fit in. She needs to find her place, and if her behavior is bad, she never will. Life can be lonely when you're an outsider. Even for horses."

Right then, I felt like Scrooge getting visits from the past, present, and future. "Are you trying to give me a message, too?"

He tilted his hat back, giving me an unobstructed view of the blue eyes Megan fell in love with. "Am I trying?" He looked at the ground and kicked at the dirt. "No. But you can learn a lot from animals. Was there a lesson here for you?"

I gnawed on my cheek and his question. Was there a lesson? "I suppose there's a lesson in everything."

"You're right about that." He tipped his hat forward and jumped the gate again. Over his shoulder, he said, "If you really want to see something interesting, Roland is in the breeding barn doing an ultrasound."

The mention of Roland turned and twisted my stomach. Did I dare seek him? Would there be a lesson there, too?

Chapter 8

NATALIE

I wasn't sure how to play this. Did I walk in and pretend nothing happened last night? Everything he'd said struck a chord with me. Being accused of carrying a transmittable disease was bad, but describing me as a project was worse. The words hurt.

Maybe it was Roland who needed to be harnessed and taken to the arena for an adjustment, and I'd be happy to be his trainer.

When I turned the corner, I saw something no person should have to see: Roland had his entire arm buried inside a horse's ass.

The sight was disturbing and funny and the same time. He was buried so deep, he'd become part of the horse's ass—very fitting.

He craned his head over his shoulder to see me standing in the doorway. "I'm glad you're here."

He was glad I was here? Did that mean he'd apologize? "I'm here because Killian said you were doing something interesting and I should check it out." I walked closer. Yep, he was buried to his shoulder. "If you wanted to check her throat, I'm pretty sure it would have been easier to go through her mouth."

He rolled his eyes. "I need you to wiggle the wire. I got a few shots taken, but the damn thing seems to have shorted out."

I went over to the small television screen, shook its wire, and

Set Up

watched it come to life. Pulsing through the air was a heartbeat, and on the screen something moved. "That's her baby?" I asked with awe. I'd never seen life like this.

"Yes, ma'am. He's looking good. This is the last look I'll take unless something goes wrong. It's not comfortable for her or me." He pressed a button in his free hand, and still images began to collect as thumbnails on the screen.

"That's amazing." I bent in front of the screen and looked at all the pictures.

"You want to be next?" A sucking sound was followed by a pop. "I've got a clean glove."

My butt cheeks clenched. Bolting to an upright position, I spun around so he no longer had a view of my ass. "So now you're being funny. I'm not sure which is more endearing, you accusing me of having chlamydia, or you threatening to check my tonsils through my ass."

"I never said you had chlamydia."

"You said you weren't looking for an STD, and since it's the most common, I figured that was what you meant."

"You seem to know a great deal about sexually transmitted diseases." He peeled the glove from his arm and tossed it into a metal tub in the corner, then went to the sink to scrub up.

"Why are you so mean to me?"

He pulled a paper towel from the dispenser and dried off. "Listen, Natalie, we got off to a bad start. Can we try again?"

"Are you going to be mean?"

"It's not my intention. Are you going to be annoying?"

I lifted my shoulders and shrugged. "Probably. Annoying is my specialty."

"Good to know."

My eyes locked with his, and there were no words that could summarize my intense desire for this man. There was no explanation either. Sure he was sexy, but he wasn't nice.

"The girls called you the nice guy."

He let out a throat-clearing growl. "That statement is the kiss of death."

"It's also a lie." I followed him back to the stall and the horse he'd recently violated. "You've got them fooled. You're not nice at all."

He turned to me, and his right brow bounced up. "What makes you think it's a lie?" In a lover's voice, he coaxed the horse out of the stall and led her toward the door.

It took two of my steps to keep up with his one. "First, you hurt my feelings. Second, you hurt my feelings. Third—"

"I hurt your feelings." He clucked at the horse, and she nudged his cheek with hers.

"No. Third, you had your hand stuck up a horse's ass, and that had to hurt her."

His laugh filled the air around us, its deep warmth filling every cold, empty spot in me.

"She didn't seem to mind." He ran his hand up the neck of the horse. To my disbelief, she nuzzled closer to him.

I fisted up and popped him in the arm. "Isn't that uncomfortable for them?"

"Given the choice, I'm sure she wouldn't volunteer to have my arm up her ass, but we lost a foal not too long ago due to an umbilical cord problem, and I needed to make sure her pregnancy was solid."

We made our way to the stables, where Keagan relieved him of the horse. Keagan looked from Roland to me and gave us a cat-got-the-mouse smile. Then his look turned serious. "Everything okay with the foal?" He held still. Not breathing. Waiting.

"It's all right as rain."

A whoosh of air raced from him. He took in a deep breath and relaxed. Every muscle in his body softened in relief. "Yes!" He threw both fists in the air, celebrating the good news.

"I don't see anything that should cause us concern."

Keagan patted the mare's neck and spoke words of encouragement and praise.

"I'm out of here," Roland said.

"Barbecue tomorrow. Mickey wants to fine tune the event. You coming?"

Set Up

Roland looked at the ground and shuffled his boots in the dirt. His blue eyes traveled from the dust up my body and landed on my lips. What felt like an hour of staring ended with a clipped reply. "Nope."

"I'll let her know." Keagan turned and disappeared into the stables with the horse.

My heart jolted in my chest. It didn't take a genius to figure out I was the reason for his planned absence, but I didn't understand why. What was it about me that repulsed him?

"Roland?" He almost made it to his truck before I caught up with him.

He turned to face me, but not before I heard him sigh. Not since I was a little girl nipping at the heels of my mom's Louboutins had I heard that sound.

"What's up, Natalie?" Even my name was spoken with aggravation.

"Can I ask you a question?"

He tilted his head and thinned his lips. "Doesn't look like I'm getting a choice here."

My arms tightened around my middle. "Why do you hate me?"

He lowered his head and looked at the ground. "I don't hate you. I just don't have any use for you."

Anger curled hot and unstoppable in my gut, like a blazing inferno that wanted to burn that sexy blond hair straight from his big, fat head.

"And I thought you were nice, and sexy, and—"

His eyes grew wide at my rage. "And what?"

"Worth my time."

"Your time? What time is that, Natalie? The few minutes you'd give me between now and when you move on with your life?" Roland took the last two strides to his truck. "Not interested, sweetheart."

"You're not nice, Roland, and you're a liar. Stop eye-fucking me every time you see me if you're not interested." I swiped at the tear running down my cheek and took off toward my cabin.

Inside, I collapsed on the couch and cried. Everyone wanted to hurt me, it seemed: Mom, Rosa, Mickey, and now Roland. I'd walked into prison everyone's princess but had walked out a pariah.

The front door rattled with a thump. *What now?* I'd already been hanged and drawn. Was this the person sent to quarter me?

I scrubbed my hands over my face and trudged to the door. Holly stood on the porch with a bag of burgers in one hand, a half-gallon of ice cream in the other, and a warm smile on her face.

Burgers, ice cream, or a hug from Holly—I didn't know which I needed more. But I knew I'd take all three; I could decide later which one was most effective.

The door swung wide, and I pulled her inside. "Hurry, close the door before anything else befalls me."

Holly headed straight for the kitchen and set down the goodies. "Mickey called and told me she'd been hard on you," she said, pulling plates from the cupboard.

I pulled a spoon from the drawer and peeled off the top of the chocolate chunky monkey ice cream and dug in. Cold and creamy, it soothed the heated hurt I felt at Roland's words. It softened the blow I'd received from Mickey, and it sweetened the bitterness I felt toward my mother.

Holly pulled the container and the spoon away from me. "Real food first. Junk later." She pressed a plate loaded with a burger and fries into my hand, grabbed her own, and took a seat at the small dining table.

"You're going to make a great mom."

"All I can do is my best." She patted her belly and smiled.

"What does it feel like to have a person growing inside you?"

I nibbled on the fries the way a rabbit does a carrot. It was a habit I'd had since I was a kid. Tiny little bites savored one by one until they were gone.

"It's amazing. Keagan and I created this life from love. He or she grows every day, and I get to watch this little human take shape."

Had my mom felt the same way, or had she been despondent because Prada didn't make maternity clothes? "What if he or she doesn't turn out to be who you expected?"

Holly took a bite of her burger. I wasn't sure whether she was digesting the question or the food, but it took her a while to respond. "Are we talking about my child or you?"

"Neither." Her brow raised in a don't-lie-to-me fashion. "Both."

"I can't speak for your mom. My only hope is that with love and encouragement, my child turns out to be who they want to be."

I bit into my burger and reflected on my upbringing. I was a diamond, and with that came expectations—damn my own dreams. I had to dream what was expected. It was how I became an accountant. It was how I could host a hundred people on a minute's notice, but I couldn't boil an egg. I was raised with core values that reflected wealth, position, and power. It wasn't who you were that counted; it was what you had.

"Why does everyone hate me?" I was the lone attendee to my very own pity party.

"No one hates you."

"Oh, yes they do. My mom hates me. Mickey is disgusted with me, and Roland…oh, my God, Roland despises me."

Holly's brows puckered. "Roland doesn't despise anyone, he's a ni—"

I pressed my finger to her lips. "Don't you dare say nice guy. He's not nice at all. He told me he has no use for me."

"Really?" Holly's head tilted back and forth like a metronome set to slow. "He said that?"

"Yes, and last night he told me he wasn't interested in getting an STD or taking on a project."

Holly laughed.

"This isn't funny. He attacked my character. He hurt my feelings."

"What? Are you six?"

"You're taking his side?"

"No, I'm saying rather than sit here and stew, prove him wrong. Obviously, you like him, or your feelings wouldn't be hurt."

I dipped my head in embarrassment. I did like him, and it drove me bat-shit crazy. I could have any man in the world, and the one I wanted was the one who didn't want me in return. "Maybe I'm attracted to the challenge. You know, like when someone tells you you can't have something and you get it anyway to prove them wrong?"

Holly shook her head. "I was never like that. If I was told I couldn't have something, I assumed there was a good reason for the decision."

That was an odd concept for me. "I was the opposite." I always pushed the envelope.

"Not surprising." She took our empty plates and put them in the sink, then came back to sit down. Yep, Holly was born to be a mother. "What about your mom?"

I told her about our exchange and how Mom had raced around the house avoiding me. I complained about the car, my lack of money, and showed her the watch that started it all. Finally, it was on my wrist, where it belonged all along. Then I exhaled and faced the truth.

"She hates me."

Holly reached over and touched my hand. It was a soft caress that said she cared. "She doesn't hate you. I bet she hates herself."

"Yes, for having me."

She raised her hand to cup my cheek. "Natalie, not everything that happens is about you."

I leaned back, and her hand fell from my face. "Now you sound like Mickey."

"Are you listening to everyone, or are you actually hearing them? There is a difference."

"You make me sound like a spoiled brat."

"You are. But you're lovable, and you have so much to offer others if you'd just get out of your own way."

"What does that even mean?"

"Look deep inside yourself and find out what's in there. You're more than brand names and baubles. You're more than your mom's minimal expectations."

"Minimal? I was whatever she asked me to be at the time."

"Exactly, and you never got to develop into you."

"So, I really am six."

Set Up

She shrugged. "Maybe."

"Great, I'm six going on twenty-six. No wonder Roland isn't interested. I make him feel like a pedophile."

"When he looks at you, he sees a woman. Now show him the woman you are, not the woman you want him to think you are."

"I have no idea who I am."

"Isn't it time you found out?" She rose from her chair and leaned over to hug me. "I gotta go. I left a bag of burgers on the counter for Keagan, and he'll be wondering where I disappeared to."

I looked at the woman in front of me. She was peaceful, content, and happy. "What does it feel like to be in love?"

She closes her eyes and hummed. "It's like being wrapped in twelve hundred count sheets and fed chocolate mousse."

Now it was my time to laugh. "That sounds pretty damn divine." I walked with her to the door and gave her another hug.

"Eat that container of ice cream and then make a plan. Every girl needs a plan."

I did have a plan. "I'm getting a dog."

"That sounds like fun. You should talk to Roland about breeds and stuff." She winked at me.

"Sure," I said, knowing I wouldn't.

Down the steps and into the fading light of day she disappeared, but her words remained with me. *You never got to develop into you.*

Reinvent myself? That was my specialty. Find my authentic self? That was impossible. Nothing good happened when I started from scratch.

In the distance, the sun was setting, washing the cabins in a fiery orange, much like the cake I caught on fire when I was eleven—another failed attempt at domestication.

As for Roland, he didn't have any use for me, or I for him. The floorboards creaked under my feet and echoed in the silence. It had been a long time since I'd been alone. With the door closed and locked, I went straight for the half-gallon of ice cream. Tonight, it was the chocolate chunky monkey and me. What a pair.

Chapter 9

ROLAND

My truck bounced all the way to the interstate. The gravel clicked up to hit the undercarriage, threatening to chip the paint straight off, much the same way Natalie's words chipped at my resolve to stay away from her.

That damn woman had me running, and I never ran from a woman in my life. She walked into a room, and everything went to hell. My heart beat too fast. My head pounded from the rush of blood. My damn hands shook. And my dick—damn traitor—stood up and saluted her like she ruled the world.

The storm called Natalie would be fun and exciting while it lasted, but she'd blow through and leave me destroyed in its wake. Complete disaster.

Left or right, the decision was mine. Did I take the turn that led me into her storm? Could I survive someone like her? Eyes like a fine whiskey. Voice like a summer breeze. Hair the color of rich soil. I yanked the steering wheel left and drove to Rick's. What couldn't be solved in the moment could be contemplated over a beer.

I walked into pure chaos. Friday nights at Rick's were a different beast altogether. Weekdays, the men outnumbered the women, but on weekends, the ratio was two to one in my favor. At the bar, I slipped into the only open stool and slapped a ten on the worn wood surface.

"Give me a tall."

Rick's eyes widened. "Friday night?" He pulled a chilled glass from under the bar and lowered the tap with a touch of his thumb.

"Just needed a change of scenery." I reached for the cup of stale nuts and picked out the spicy peanuts, popping them into my mouth one at a time, letting the burn settle in my stomach.

"Where you been?"

Rick was somewhere between sixty and dead. He'd been in my life forever. Dad brought me here to drink my first beer. Since then I'd made a stop every week but rarely on a Friday. Too many people. Too many games.

"Where I always am. I held clinic hours today, though, so the ranch was the smallest part of my day—but it was the most frustrating part."

Rick poured himself a shot of top-shelf whiskey, a perk of owning a bar and living in a house out back. He could stumble to his bunk without worry.

"Problem with a filly?"

Her face was clear in his mind. Cheeks red with rage. Eyes normally brown now colored black with hate. *Problem with a filly?* "Yep. The two-legged kind."

Rick's laughter started low in his gut and worked its way up to an out-of-season *oh ho ho*. "Told you she was trouble."

The beer went down smoothly and quickly, but it failed to cool the heat burning inside me. "I hardly know her, and she's under my skin like a developing rash I can't cure." My glass disappeared, and another full, frosted mug took its place.

"Attraction happens that way."

"Attraction? More like repellent. She's pretty, I'll give her that, but she knows it. That's the trouble."

Rick moved down the bar to help another patron, but I kept on with my diatribe on all the reasons Natalie Diamond was bad news.

"She's too forward. Hell, she offered herself up that first night." Rather than sip my beer, I guzzled it. "It was an appealing offer.

Damn appealing. Visions of her boots on my shoulders tortured me all damn night."

"I'm back. What's this about boots on your shoulders?" Rick picked up my sweating mug and wiped the condensation pooling on the table.

"Remember back in grammar school when you liked a girl and you would hit her or call her names to get her attention?"

"You're askin' me to remember a lifetime ago, son. What's your point?"

"I accused her of having an STD and slapped her with the title of being too much work."

The tip of the wet towel stung as it flicked my head. Rick was winding up for another snap when I reached out and snatched the bar towel from his hands.

"What are you, eight?"

"Would seem so. She riles me up, Rick. She unsettles me." I tossed the wet towel back to the old man.

He looked past me to the bar door. His Sam Elliot mustache turned up into a smile. "Your world is about to get a bit more unstable." He poured a shot of his private stash and slid it across the counter. "Drink up, boy. You're going to need it."

She was here. I knew it. Maybe it was the look on Rick's face that said it all, or maybe it was the buzz that vibrated through my body the second she walked in. Or maybe that was the beer.

Determined to not look, I sat as still as a granite statue and stared at the wall of liquor bottles in front of me. She walked up, and her face reflected on every shiny piece of glass behind the bar. Damn Rick for being such a neat freak. She smiled and ordered a glass of wine.

"House Merlot, please." Her voice ran over my body like simple syrup cascading over me and dripping into my senses.

Rick popped the cork on a fresh bottle and poured her a glass. I sat still, facing the bar. Out of the corner of my eye, I watched her plop down a bill.

"This one's on Roland here." Rick slapped the space in front of me. Every eye in the place turned my way. "I hear he owes you

Set Up

one." He pushed the bill back toward her. "Take it as an apology for his primate behavior."

She forced the bill back toward Rick. "No, thank you. I'm monkeyed out tonight."

He stuck the bill into the register and counted back change for a hundred. "Pull up a chair, darlin'." Then he cuffed me on the ear. "Give the girl your chair, asshole."

What happened to me between last night and today? I never would have left a girl standing. "Sorry. Here you go, Natalie." The metal legs of the old bar stool scraped and whined across the wood floor until I positioned it behind her. "Fabulous ass," I said on an exhale. Two beers and a shot had loosened my tongue.

"Excuse me?" She whipped her head around to look at my eyes glued to her ass.

Hand over my mouth, I coughed. "I said sorry for being an ass."

"Why apologize for something you excel at?" She wrapped two fingers around the stem of the glass and swirled it like a pro. It rose like a wave to the edge without spilling, then calmed to a mirror-like finish.

"I deserve that." I raised my hand to Rick, signaling for another drink. He shook his head and poured me a cup of coffee.

"You're right. You did." She raised her glass. "Shall we toast?"

My chest grazed her shoulder when I leaned over her to pick up the cup of coffee that looked more like mud than brew.

"What are we toasting to?"

"Yesterday, when you were doctoring my knees, I asked you if you were a proctologist."

"I believe that's correct." Where in the hell was she going with this line of questioning?

She raised her glass and touched the edge of my mug. "To you, Roland. You found your calling. Asses to elbows, you said. Looks like you've mastered the art, but not the balance. At this point, I'm not sure what's embedded deeper—your arm up a horse's ass, or your head up yours." She looked down at the stool I vacated moments before. "I won't be needing your chair."

And with a toss of her hair, she disappeared into the crowd.

"How'd it go?"

"Like a fart in church." I sipped at the black sludge and eyed the crowd, trying to find the one woman who made me want to kiss her as much as choke her.

"I did that once. It's a forgivable offense." Rick scouted the room like a pro. "Three o'clock by the wall—stallions moving in."

I flipped around so fast, my head spun. Holding up the dark paneling, looking around the room, stood Natalie. Every few seconds her eyes caught mine, and then she glanced away, but her eyes always came back to me. I knew that for certain because mine never left her.

Man after man approached her. She smiled and chatted for a minute, then sent them on their way. It didn't appear she was offering to be nice to any of those men.

Had it really been me she was interested in, and not just a random dick?

My cock jumped at the notion. I turned around and leaned against the bar. The whole night could be spent watching her. So much could be learned about a person when they weren't switched on. For instance, when she smiled, she was only being polite. It didn't reach her eyes, only stayed on her lips until the person passed. Her eyes danced with mischief last night but were dull under strain today.

Did I cause that?

Dressed in a pair of jeans and a pink shirt, she wasn't made up like the others in the bar. No big hair, no makeup, no pretense. Natalie hadn't come here to find someone; she'd come here for the same reason I did: to escape.

I pushed from the bar and started toward her. A young cowboy wannabe pulled on her arm, trying to force her to the dance floor.

Step by step, I closed the gap. My strides grew longer as her discomfort grew.

"No," she said and yanked her arm back. "I told you I don't want to dance."

"Listen, you bi—"

I poked the man on his back. "The lady said she doesn't want to dance." My fingers wrapped around the collar of his shirt and yanked him back, making him stumble on his snakeskin boots. "Move on, asshole."

"You're calling me an asshole in front of the lady?"

"I am, and this lady is an expert in assholes. What do you say, Natalie? Does he meet the criteria for being an asshole?"

A spark of life shone in her eyes—a little glimmer of energy that had been missing before.

Her ripe lips lifted into a heart-stopping smile. "He's just a beginner but well on his way."

With a push, I released the guy's shirt and sent him staggering forward. "Move on, little asshole, she prefers the big ones."

One step forward, and I had her pressed to the wood paneling. My mouth was on hers like tape on paper. She smelled like fresh oranges and tasted like wine and trouble. Our kiss was a battle; our mouths, the battlefield. Her tongue challenged and fought me. Each time I pulled away, she gripped my shoulders and brought me back into the war we waged against each other.

"You're an asshole," she panted into my mouth.

"I know." I sucked on her lower lip until it grew hot, plump and red.

"You're mean."

"I can be." My hands threaded through her hair and held her where I wanted her—head tugged back and looking at me with glazed eyes.

"I hate you." She pulled my lower lip between her teeth and bit. Hard.

I ran my tongue across the swelling flesh and tasted a hint of metal. "You should."

"Why are you kissing me?" She pressed her hands to my chest. First with a push, then they slid to explore me from shoulders to belt.

I pulled back and ran my thumb over her swollen lower lip. "It stops me from wanting to kill you."

"Keep kissing me, then. I'm not ready to die."

"Natalie, you and I are like ice and fire. We don't belong together, but I'll be damned if I can stay away from you."

Her scent drove me crazy. Oranges and vanilla ice cream filled my senses. I buried my lips in the crease of her neck, ran my tongue along her collarbone, and swallowed the shiver that raced through her body.

"Yes, we're dark and light, good and bad, and so wrong, it's right."

She unbuttoned my shirt and ran her palm over my chest. Every hair stood up and took notice. Hot and throbbing, my cock pressed against her stomach.

"What are we doing?" I ground against her, trying to find relief.

"We're negotiating a truce." Her ragged breath tickled the skin she exposed. Desire rippled across my skin like a wave.

Keys jingled above us. "You two want my room for a bit? Changed the sheets last week." Rick held his key ring above our heads and shook it like a bell.

"Shit, Rick." I stepped back and sucked in a breath of clarity.

"I can't have you two going at it over here against the wall. It's against the health code."

Natalie couldn't get any closer to the paneling without becoming part of the grain. "I gotta go." She picked her purse up from the floor and ran for the exit.

"Damn it, Rick. Why'd you do that?" One look around the room, and I knew why. All eyes were on me. "I need to catch her."

Rick grabbed my collar like I had the asshole's earlier. "Let her go, son. She'll be thinking about you all night long. Let her think. If you chased her down, all you'd do is open your mouth and piss her off."

He had a point. This was the first time Natalie and I had been together where she didn't leave pissed. At least I hoped she wasn't pissed.

Chapter 10

NATALIE

Dust kicked up in the rearview mirror. The tires squealed and spun until they hit the firm pavement and caught traction on the asphalt. My eyes shifted between the mirror and the road. Would Roland follow me? Part of me wanted that to happen, and the rest of me wanted to hide for the next week so I wouldn't have to face him.

What the hell was I thinking? Even alcohol couldn't be blamed. One glass of wine didn't create an idiot. That, I'd done on my own. He'd kissed me into stupid while I was pressed up against the dark, wooden wall, and I'd nearly stripped him bare.

I couldn't blame it on anything but raw, hot desire, and not for anyone but Roland. A line of guys had tried their best tonight, and I'd passed on each one of them until he showed up and took what the others wanted. He didn't give me a choice. He covered my mouth with his lips, and I was a goner. I would've liked to say I fought a good fight or made him work for it, but that would be a lie. Not once did I push him away. If I recalled correctly, my hands had been all over his body, and I'd pulled him toward me.

Who the hell am I? That seemed to be the subject of the moment. All these years I'd inhabited this body, and I still didn't have a clue.

Miles past Rick's Roost, the car eased into the blackness of the night. Two left turns and one right turn brought me onto the county road that would lead me home. Home, not the mansion in Cherry Creek, but the little cabin I hardly took notice of.

The hatchback was no match for a four-wheeling road. It bounced and lurched over the pocked and pitted ground. White-knuckling the steering wheel, I sat forward with my chin above the dash. No street lamps—only the headlights and soft glow of the ranch in the distance to guide me.

A flash of fur stopped in front of the car. With a yank of the steering wheel to the right, the car rocketed off the gravel road and slipped into the shallow ravine, where it came to an abrupt stop.

Jarred, I sat for a moment, trying to figure out what happened. I had been on the road—and now I wasn't.

I threw open the door and ran to the road to make sure I hadn't hurt the deer. The glow of the headlights shed enough light for me to see it was gone. I would have died if I'd killed Bambi. A final glance around confirmed it. No bloody carcass, just an empty, dark road ahead.

I threw my hands in the air and screamed, "What else?"

Daddy had always told me to not to go looking for trouble, but trouble was a stalker hot on my heels.

Fifteen minutes later, I was still trying to get my car out of the damn ditch. A storm had evidently hit recently, judging from the standing water that had turned the dirt into a thick sludge. Every time I pressed the gas pedal, the car whistled, whined, and sunk deeper into the ground.

Without a phone, I couldn't call for help. I'd have to rescue myself. What an odd concept. I had never been without options—until now. I turned off the lights and closed the door, not bothering to lock it. Let someone steal this heap of junk. Getting it out of the ditch would be a huge boon for me.

Pitch black, the night curled around me. Step by step, I stumbled down the rocky road. Sounds came at me like snipers' bullets. A hoot from the left. A hiss from the right. Blood pounded in my head. Its cadence set the pace for home. Men were all over me in the bar, but where were they when I really needed one? Where was Roland? Was he still at the bar, now playing tonsil hockey with another girl? A rustle in the trees, and thoughts of Roland disappeared. My heart raced—a pace so fast, my feet had a hard time keeping up with the rhythm. A shadow up ahead stopped me dead. Fisting the handle of my purse, I held it like a club, ready to bludgeon anyone or anything who stood between me and my home. Robyn would be proud.

"I've had a damn bad day, so whatever you are, move on!" I yelled, squinting to see in the darkness.

A fox emerged from the shrubs, the shadow of its long, bushy tail my only clue to its identity. Under the low light of the moon, it looked at me with interest, then turned and walked away.

"That's right. Keep on moving." Were the words for me or the fox? Either way, they worked. I continued my quick clip up the barren road toward the lit-up farmhouse. The howl to my right moved me from a power walk to a run. There was no way I was going to let myself get eaten by a wolf or coyote after surviving three years of prison.

With my eyes glued to the end cabin, I bolted like a sprinter until I was up the stairs and inside the door. Back pressed against the solid wood, I slid to the floor and gulped in air.

I made it. I cheated death.

The feeling of accomplishment washed over me. This wasn't my life. I was out of my comfort zone. This was worse than prison. Prison was predictable. Life on this ranch was not, but I'd survived it so far. I dragged myself to a standing position and kicked off my shoes. The thick carpet massaged my sore feet.

In the center of the room was a wall of blue. The bins taunted me with their presence. Did I dare open them? They contained all that remained of my past life. Could I face the sober reminder of everything I once had?

Negotiating with myself, I stood in front of the first bin and shook it. No clanks, no clicks, no clatter, just the soft swish of fabric. The sound was safe.

The lid broke free with a twist and a tug. Inside was an entire store of lingerie. Bras. Underwear. Thigh-highs. Pajamas. Who knew old underwear could bring me such joy?

Small folded pieces of silk surrounded the floor where I sat. I rose and took the little bundles to my bedroom. A room I had only given a passing glance. I dressed and slept there, and that was all.

On closer inspection, I noticed a candle sat on the nightstand. Its pine scent filled the air. The bedding had been selected with me in mind. Gold, tan, and brown were my favorite colors, and they decorated the room from the curtains to the throw pillows.

Above the bed was an inscription: *Life isn't about finding yourself. Life is about creating yourself.* Under it was the name George Bernard Shaw.

I leaned over and traced the letters with my fingers. Who was I? No, that was wrong, according to Mr. Shaw. The real question was: who did I want to be?

Right now, I wanted to be invisible. My friend had opened her life to me and provided me with a home, yet I wasn't taking the time to look at how much she had really given me. Without her, I'd be living in the housekeeper's car.

Mickey made this place special for me. When was the last time someone had done something that nice just for me?

Lined up like scoops of ice cream, a rainbow of colors filled the top drawer of my dresser. Thoughts of ice cream made me think of the half gallon of chocolate chunky monkey I'd eaten. When that didn't make me feel better, I'd thought wine would. That led me to Rick's Roost, and Roland, and that kiss.

I shed my clothes and slid on some flannel boxer shorts and a T-shirt. The material caressed my skin the way I hoped Roland would. What would happen the next time I saw him? Would he pull me into his arms for more, or would he pretend that amazing kiss never happened?

"We don't belong together," he'd told me.

That was right after he kissed the sense out of me, and right before he seemed ready to take me against the wall. My skin prickled at the memory of his hands on my body. I needed a splash of cold water or a case of amnesia. Too bad the former was my only realistic option.

In the bathroom, I took a good look at myself. My hair had grown long in prison. It now lay softly below my shoulders. My skin was nice, and my teeth were perfect thanks to early intervention.

"I'd do me," I said to my reflection, then grimaced. *I'm resorting to talking to myself?*

The silence threw me off. The hum of the refrigerator filled the air. If I listened close enough, the outside came in with the hoots of an owl, the chirp of crickets, and the whistle of the wind as it raced between the buildings. I ventured into the living room I hadn't picked up since yesterday. That's why I didn't eat at home—hardly stayed there, in fact. If you lived in your house, you were obligated to tidy it up.

Once the bottles and cans were picked up in the living room, I eyed the tower of blue bins again. "I'm coming back for you tomorrow." I shut off the lights and headed to bed.

Soft sheets kissed my skin, and the comforter hugged my body. Sad that the best hug I got all day came from my bedding.

Shadows danced across the ceiling. Funny images played with my mind. The ditch. Roland. The deer. Roland. A dog. Roland. It kept coming back to Roland.

I flopped on my side and closed my eyes. Tomorrow would be a better day.

I'd give Mickey a hug for giving me a place in her heart and her home.

I'd get my car out of the ditch.

I'd get a dog.

I'd get one step closer to my inheritance.

Chapter 11

NATALIE

Someone would die today.
Ka-bam
Neigh
Clippity clop
Ka-bam

I covered my head and buried myself deeper into the mattress, but not even a thick comforter could muffle the sounds of a working ranch.

Ka-bam
Ka-bam
Ka-bam

Each boom was like a strike to my head. If Toby didn't stop pounding nails into that damn fence, my fingers were destined to wrap around his neck and squeeze the last living breath from his body.

Car doors slammed, and voices caught on the breeze. The squeal of a young girl split the air. Then came the pounding on my door.

Ratty-haired and sleepy-eyed, I walked like a drunk to the front of the house and flung open the door.

Set Up

"What?"

Cole leaned against the doorjamb, arms crossed in front of his body. The Stetson sat back on his head, showing off blue eyes that undoubtedly made girls swoon. They were all wrong. Not the darker than Tiffany blue I loved, but the blue of a clear morning sky. Pretty enough, but they didn't make my panties wet.

"Saw your car in a ditch down the road. You okay?"

All the hot air left me. It was hard staying mad at a guy who only cared about my safety.

"Avoided a deer and fell off the edge."

"Deer can be a nuisance. The fire last year destroyed their natural terrain, and they've moved into populated areas." He scanned my body from head to toe. "Sure you're all right?"

I held out my arms and spun in a circle. "Does it look like I'm okay?"

A smile stole across his face. "You look better than okay."

"Down, boy." I leaned forward and flicked off his hat. "Can you help me get my car out of the ditch?"

Cole reseated his hat and held out his hands. "Give me your keys. Tyson and I will get it for you."

"You sure?"

"Give me your keys." His annoyance was an act. His big-ass smile showed his true emotions.

I turned and ran toward the coffee table. "Thank you. You want some coffee or something when you get back?"

That was all I had to offer him. My finances were limited, and I didn't cook, so there were no cakes or cookies, but I could shove a pod in a coffee pot and push start.

"You want me to have coffee with you or get your car? You only get to choose one. Daylight's burning."

The keys left my hands and flew through the air.

Perfect throw.

Perfect catch.

"Car it is, or we can go for that *something* you mentioned." His eyes rose with his hopes.

"Get the car." Eye rolls were becoming a thing with me.

He turned on his boots and left.

Back in the kitchen, I brewed a cup of morning gold. The girls were right. This little machine was like a personal Starbucks. It spit and sputtered until the cup was full. There was nothing like this in the prison cafeteria. Our coffee was the color of tea and tasted like dishwater.

Moments later, my little white car was pulling up in front of my cabin. Cole unfolded his long body and stepped from the tiny box. I met him at the door.

"Thank you, Cole."

He pulled the cup from my hand and took a drink. "You're welcome. Doesn't look any worse for the wear. A few scratches, is all." When he handed my cup back, it was almost empty. "Got that coffee after all. Next time, I'll take two sugars and a dash of milk."

"I'll keep that in mind."

"By the way…" He peered over his shoulder toward the other cabins. "I'm in five, Toby is in four, and Tyson is in three. Holly is in seven now that she's living with her husband, and Megan is in eight with Killian."

"Got it." I tipped back the last of the coffee and swallowed the sweetest bit.

"I'm in five," he said again. Light glinted in his eyes. "Just in case."

"In case I crash my car again?" I lifted my brows and waited.

"That, or you need anything else." Emphasis was put on the word 'anything'.

"I do need something." Each word came out on a breathy whisper.

"Yeah?" He leaned in within inches of my mouth.

Cole's lips were pink and supple looking, but thinner than Roland's and not as appetizing.

"Will Roland be around today?" My voice caught and rose an octave despite my attempt at controlled indifference.

Cole's head snapped back. "Roland?"

"Yes. I'm getting a dog, and I thought he could answer a few questions."

Set Up

Cole nodded. "Right." He dropped my keys in my hand. "Roland should be here for the barbecue. You're coming, right?"

I nodded. "Yes, I'll be there. I want to contribute." Genius—another opportunity to make a difference. I could double down. Saving a dog and helping the ranch. Mom couldn't overlook that.

"See you tonight." He tipped his hat and left.

DRESSED in a pair of sexy silk panties covered by hand-me-down jeans and a gypsy top, I slipped on a pair of flats and went in search of Mickey.

The dirt parking lot was full. Strangers on horses trotted by with smiles on their faces. Cole, Tyson, and Toby were helping people saddle up, while Mickey checked things off a clipboard.

She saw me coming and gave me a weak smile. "Have you come to murder me?" She dropped her hands next to her body and swung the clipboard back and forth.

A soft giggle erupted from me. "No, I've come to thank you."

Everything from her eyes to her lips slanted. "You're thanking me for handing you your ass?"

"No, for that I want to kill you." I wrapped my arm around her shoulder and pulled her in next to me for a hug. "Just kidding," I sang. "Actually, I wasn't happy about it, but you aren't saying anything I haven't heard—especially lately. The last two days have been the same sledgehammer against my head."

"And you survived. You'll be okay. What's up with you today?" A young girl led her horse out of the stables and past Mickey. "Have a good ride, Shayla," she called after the horse and rider.

"Why's it so busy today?"

"Weekend. All the boarders come to ride. Now that it's spring and the snow is mostly melted, it will be a zoo here most weekends." She patted the hind end of a big black horse that walked by with a rider. "You're welcome to take a ride anytime you like. Just ask one of the guys, and they'll saddle up a mount for you."

"The last time I rode a horse, I was still wearing a training bra."

I cupped my boobs and gave them a little shake. "That was a long time ago."

"I'm sure I could get one of the guys to get you in the saddle again."

"I think I'm okay for now. When it comes to animals, I'm going to start smaller. Which is why I'm here. I was going to get a dog, but I wanted to ask you first if that's okay."

Mickey dropped the clipboard and scrambled to pick it up. "You're going to get a dog?" Her voice bubbled with laughter. "You know they poop, right?"

It was an unfortunate aspect of pet ownership. "Yes, I know they poo."

"They need to be fed, and walked, and bathed."

"Maybe I should have just gotten one and begged for forgiveness rather than permission."

"No, asking means you're maturing. A dog, huh? Why?"

Oh shit. Here she thought I was maturing, and maybe I was in some things, but I didn't have the answer she wanted to hear. It wasn't because I loved dogs. It was a means to an end. When I was finished, I'd find it a good—permanent—home.

"I really need this, Mickey." There wasn't anything fake in my pleading tone. My need for a dog outweighed everything, even orgasms.

"Okay, but there are a few conditions. You need to control your animal. Some of the horses can be skittish around dogs. You need to clean up after it, too. I don't want to step on a pile of dog shit one time."

The woman trounced through horse shit every day, and she was concerned about a little dog doo? "Deal."

"Dogs require a lot of care and attention. It will be good for you to have to look after something."

"I want to make a difference." The main difference I was aiming for would be found in my bank account. "Speaking of differences, I'll take over the books for the Junior Rodeo thing you got going on. It's been years since I've done anything, as you know, but I'm sure I can figure out what you need."

Set Up

Mickey jumped up and hooted. "You have no idea how happy that makes me." She danced around me like a loon. "I hate the paperwork. Kerrick will be so happy to see my face again. Generally, I lock myself inside the office for hours at night." She hugged me tightly, digging the clipboard into my back. "I'll pay you what I can."

"You gave me a home and your family. I couldn't take any money from you." *Besides, I won't need it in a few weeks.* "Do you want me to work out of your office?"

"Do you have a computer?"

Did I? "I'm not sure. I suppose there could be one in the bins. I'll look later. No matter what, I'll take a look at things tomorrow and get started for sure on Monday."

"I'm so proud of you, Natalie." Her face showed the same expression it did when she talked about the ranch and horses. The softness she showed when she talked about Kerrick was there, too. She was proud, and I'd do my best to keep her that way. "Do you need money?"

I did need money—lots of it. "No, Mom put a little in an envelope. She sold my stuff to pay my legal fees. What was left, she gave to me. I also got this back." I raised my wrist and showed off my watch.

"Wow, are you sure it's legally yours? What if they report it missing again?"

She was right. "Oh no. Would they do that?" I'd assumed it was mine, but what if it was a setup?

"Is there a way you can check?"

I unfastened the watch and looked at the serial number on the back. "Can I use your computer?"

"Knock yourself out. Go into the house, head left into the hallway, turn right, and take your first left. It's powered up already."

I stood still for a moment. "You trust me in your office alone?"

"Is there a reason I shouldn't?" A horse and rider passed us on their way back to the stables. "How was your ride?" Mickey asked the man.

"Excellent," the rider said and was helped into the stable by Toby.

"No. I just…"

"You just what, Natalie? I know you stole that watch, but you admitted it. That shows you're more honest than most. Get your ass in my office, and make sure you're not going back to jail anytime soon. I can't afford bail." She swatted my ass with her clipboard and sent me off to her house.

When I got to the door, I walked right in. Sitting at the table was Kerrick.

"Oh, hi. I didn't expect you here."

"Come on in." He waved me inside. "I'm finishing up my reports. What do you need?"

I'd never been nervous around guys, but Kerrick unsettled me. Maybe it was because he was a detective. Maybe it was because I knew he'd done a background check on me. Maybe it was because he most likely knew more about me than I knew about myself.

"Mickey said I could use her computer." I held up my wrist. "My watch was returned to me, but Mickey brought up a good point. What if they claim it was stolen again?"

Kerrick frowned. "Come here, Natalie." He had that same no-nonsense tone his brothers did. "Did your mom give it to you?" He cocked his head to the right.

"I don't know. It was in the glove compartment of my car with a note from my cousin saying, 'Was it worth it?'"

"And you didn't think that was odd?"

In hindsight, I supposed it was, but what had mattered to me in the moment was that I had it back. "Um…I guess. I was just so happy to see it."

"How are you going to check it?" He pushed his paperwork back and pulled his computer forward.

"Cartier has a database." I had no idea how I'd get to it, but I hoped someone at Cartier could help.

"Tell you what. You leave that watch with me for a bit, and I'll check it out." He held out his hand.

I ran my fingers over the diamonds on the face of the watch. "Really?"

"No, I'm going to steal it and pawn it. What do you think I can get for it?"

At first, I wasn't sure what to believe. He held a deadpan expression. "Ha ha, you joke. Well, if you decide to go through with the stealing and pawning, this is a Cartier Hypnose and goes for about $40,000. You can hock it, but the Cartier store in Cherry Creek Mall does buybacks, and you'll get more there." I undid the leather band and handed over my treasure.

Kerrick looked the watch over and whistled. "That's quite a watch. Why do you think your grandmother promised it to you and left it to your cousin?"

That had been the question of the day for over three years. "I have no idea, but maybe the lesson was don't believe everything you hear. Or maybe it was that life isn't fair."

"Both good lessons to learn. You're coming to the barbecue, right?"

"Yes, I'll be there."

"Good, because there will be a big announcement."

"Oh my, are you and Mickey having a baby, too?"

"No, unless there's something you know that I don't."

"No, I just thought…"

Kerrick shuffled his folders and papers forward and set my watch on top. "Where you off to?"

"I'm going to get a dog."

His head turned halfway around. "You? A dog?"

Why did everyone's head twist when I mentioned animal ownership? I let out an exasperated breath. "How hard can it be?"

"I guess you'll see. I'll bring your watch to the gathering. It's at six at the firepit."

"Do I need to bring anything?"

"Your dog." He laughed until I shut the door behind me.

Chapter 12

NATALIE

It took me an hour to find the little pet shop I'd passed a thousand times as a kid. For years, Dad and I licked the ice cream cones we bought next door and gawked in the windows, laughing at the women who walked in alone and walked out with puppies hanging out of their bag. I was one of those women today, a girl looking for a purse puppy.

Tiny fur balls sat in gilded cages that rose from the shiny wood floors. Little sweaters on tiny velvet hangers dangled from each enclosure. The perfect clothes had been matched to the puppy.

The clerk looked up, gave me a once-over, and shook her head. I'd been dismissed. Dressed like a farmer, I didn't warrant her attention. Show up here in Tahari, and she would have been all over me. Would my Cartier watch have made a difference? I felt like Julia Roberts in *Pretty Woman*. When I asked the price, would she stick her nose up at me and say, "It's very expensive"?

In the corner of the store, one puppy slept on its back, feet in the air. A sleeping puppy seemed like a safe bet.

"Excuse me?" I called.

Little Miss I Hate My Job dragged her ass toward me. "Yes?" Her voice was filled with annoyance.

Set Up

"Sorry to interrupt your day and ask you to do your job, but can you tell me how much this dog is?" I pointed to the apricot-colored dog.

"Bon Bon is $3,200. Her pedigree is good. Not quite up to Zsa Zsa's parents—" she pointed to the next cage over "—but she's decent."

"Three thousand two hundred?" My mouth hung open wide. "Does it come with a caretaker?"

"Funny."

"I'm not trying to be funny. I'm looking for a dog."

She ran her eyes down my body in the same judgmental way I'd done to others a thousand times. "Have you tried the pound?"

Her words cut into me. How often had I sliced at others in the same manner? "No, but I will. I came here to get a dog, not be treated like one or waited on by one." I whirled around, dressed in my secondhand clothes and first-class attitude. Throwing my hands up in the hair, I grabbed a line from *Pretty Woman*—"Huge mistake. Huge."—and walked out. The last laugh was on me when I climbed into the Volkswagen. Standing in the shop window was the clerk, who flipped me the bird.

The pound it was. Surely, they had some cute little thing looking for a home. I stopped at Starbucks to get a double shot nonfat vanilla latte and directions. I munched on a chocolate croissant and drove to the Dumb Friends League on Quebec Street.

In the parking lot, the sound of barking dogs bled through the walls. Dogs called out, "Come save me" to anyone within hearing range. Little did they know, one of these four-legged beasts would be saving me.

I entered the double glass doors and stood in front of the desk where a dark-haired woman sat with a smile. "Welcome. Have you been here before?" The woman reminded me of the greeter from the country club. She was warm and inviting, and I wanted to come in and stay a while.

"No." I inched closer to the counter, where she handed me a map and told me to take a look around.

"If there's a dog you're interested in, mark the cage number on the sheet."

"What are the adoption fees?"

"They vary depending on the dog, how long they've been in the system, and their particular needs."

I was down to just over $1,000. So, the dog I adopted needed to be cheap. "Okay," I said. "I'm off."

"Good luck," the friendly woman bubbled.

My slow gait took me through a chain-link labyrinth of cells. Row after row, I visited the dogs that hoped to be paroled. On the back of the map, I marked the ones that had potential. Small dogs pooped Tootsie Rolls; big dogs pooped small dogs. I'd get a small dog.

After an hour, I turned around, even though I hadn't finished the tour. Three dogs met my criteria. One was a hairless thing about the size of a boot. The second was a white fur ball with sad eyes. It looked really old, so I figured it would spend its day sleeping in the corner—easy peasy. The last dog I wrote down looked like a poodle. I wasn't in love with its orange-stained eyes, but it fit the size criteria.

I bounced back to the front counter, happy I was one step further on my journey. I laid the paper on the counter and smiled at the friendly attendant.

She plugged the information into the computer.

"The Chihuahua is four-fifty to adopt."

"Four hundred?" *I thought this was the Goodwill of pets?!*

"And fifty." She tapped on the keyboard again. "The Westie has a hold, meaning it has already been claimed by someone." More tapping. "The poodle could be a good choice for you. She's an old girl. She's already spayed, but she has doggie Parkinson's, so her vet bills will be ongoing. Is that something you can provide for her?"

"No," I said without a hint of regret. I didn't have time for sick dogs, and I didn't have a budget for vets and meds. "Isn't there a fast food dog? You know, the kind that's cheap and ready to go?"

She turned over the map and drew a big red circle around three boxes. "Look at these. They're $100 to adopt, and they're desperate for a home."

Set Up

"What's wrong with them?"

"Nothing. With the right owner, they'll be amazing. The problem is, sometimes people give up too soon. How would you feel if you did one thing wrong and your family booted you out of their life?"

I turned and started running to the marked cages. In the corner of the first was a big black dog. He lay with his head on his paws. Sad eyes looked up and then closed, as if he'd already given up. The next cage held a big, furry beast that bounced around the cage like it was an audition. The last cage was empty. I went back to the first one. The dog looked like I had felt yesterday when Mom didn't show up—dejected.

"He's a sweet boy."

The lady at the counter had crept up behind me. What was it with people these days? Make some noise, people.

"What's his name?"

"He doesn't have one. Are you willing to give him one?"

The dog lifted his head and turned it the way dogs did to squeeze your heart.

"Can I meet him first?"

She pulled a string of keys from her pocket and unlocked the door. It felt like visitation at the prison.

"Approach him slowly, and hold out your hand." She unfolded a chair that was leaning in the corner and sat it in the middle of the room. "Let him come to you."

I sat down and did as she asked. Within seconds, the dog pushed himself to a standing position and walked to me. He gave me a cautious look. Even the damn dog was judging me. Then he did something that caught me completely off guard. He sat in front of me and buried his head in my lap.

I pet his broad forehead and smoothed his velvet ears. Dogs didn't purr, but I bet this one did. He let out a sigh and relaxed against me. I was a goner. "I'll take him." It was a snap decision. He didn't meet any of the criteria.

The woman helping me gave me a monster-sized grin. "Let's go fill out the paperwork."

I leaned in and whispered, "I'll save you if you save me."

"What?" the woman asked.

"Nothing." I followed her out of the cage, and the dog lumbered back to the corner and collapsed. He was plumb spent from trying. "What would have happened to him?"

"He's set to be euthanized. We can't keep them forever."

"But he's so sweet."

"It's his breed. People don't like his breeding. Nothing he can change. You can come from a bad family and turn out great, or vice versa."

Don't I know it?

An hour later, I had a leash in my hand, a coupon for the spay and neuter clinic, and a small bag of dog food.

He followed me straight to the car and sat until I opened the door. Did I put him in the back or the front seat? This dog looked like he'd spent way too much time in the back, so I opened the passenger door and patted the stained fabric seat.

If a dog could look grateful, he did. He sat proudly in the little white brick with wheels. Its inferior brand didn't seem to bother him one bit. And there I was, a woman with a dog and a plan.

When I pulled up to the ranch, he pranced around the seat, and I remembered Mickey's warning about keeping him under control.

I pointed at him and said, "Be good. We are here by the grace of God." I hopped out of my side. "Stay," I told him. He craned his neck to see where I'd gone. His tail wagged when I showed up to his door. "Stay," I repeated as I slipped my hand through a tiny opening I'd created in the door to grab the leash. He did as I asked. This was the best dog ever. I might learn to like him.

When the door opened, he sat as if waiting for permission to leave.

Megan pulled up in front of her cabin and hopped out of a black truck. "What do you got there?"

"I brought home a dog."

"Really?"

"Shut up. We have a lot in common. I just paroled him. He wants a second chance, and I plan on giving it to him."

Set Up

She nodded her head. "Okay. What's his name?"

"I haven't decided."

"You have to call him something. What about Cujo?"

I gasped. "Uh…no." I gave him a once-over, hoping for inspiration. I got divine guidance from his black fur. "His name is Pepper." The dog's ears perked up in approval. After a scratch to his head, I tugged on his leash and Pepper jumped out. "Come on, Pepper. I'll show you your new home." His eyes took in everything around him. Cautious. I liked that. I glanced at Megan's shocked expression. "You want to come in for coffee?"

She looked around for a minute. "Sure, I got time."

The three of us entered together. Pepper tugged me to the sofa, where he lay down in front of it. I unclipped his leash and went to the kitchen to get us coffee. "Were you at work today?" I asked.

"Yes, so sad. A new girl showed up with her two babies. The kids were in one piece, but the poor girl had been beaten to a pulp. Hopefully, she makes some smart decisions in the future."

"Why would she put up with that?" I returned from the kitchen with two steaming mugs of coffee and set them both on the table.

Megan sat on the couch, her hand hung over the edge, and petted my dog. "We all put up with something."

"Yes, I put up with you for almost three years."

"You have that scenario backwards." She leaned over and picked up her cup of coffee.

"Whatever." I kicked off my shoes and dug my toes into the thick pile. I couldn't get over how good it felt. "How are things with Killian?"

Her face glowed. All the girls on the ranch got that look when their men were mentioned. "He's amazing. He wasn't easy at first, but the tough ones are worth it. Not one of the McKinleys fell easy or willingly."

"You selfish bitches," I teased. "You didn't save a McKinley for me."

"Nope, but there are other men here worth a look."

"I'll keep that in mind." The only man on my mind right now was Roland. The thought of him made me warm all over.

Megan looked at the wall of blue bins. "I like what you've done with the place. It's storage shed chic."

"It's a work in progress. I'm thinking a bin a day, and I'll be good in two weeks." What I really thought was, *Why unpack just to repack?*

Megan looked at her watch. "I gotta go. I promised to help Killian train a stallion."

"You're training horses?"

She nodded her mop of brown hair. "Crazy, right? He's training me to train them, and I like the time we spend together doing it. It's special to share that with him."

I put my finger into my mouth and pretended to gag. "You guys are making me sick."

"You're just jealous."

I gave her a nod. "Probably."

She took her empty cup to the sink and gave me a hug on her way out. "I'm proud of you, Natalie." She glanced at the sleeping dog. "He'll be good for you."

Then I was alone again. Well, not really alone—it was now Pepper and me against the world.

The bins called out to me. I could use my computer if it indeed still existed. "One bin today," I told myself. "What do you say, Pepper? Shall I open a new bin?" The dog peeled an eye open and then went back to sleep. "You're no help."

Just like last night, I shook the bins, but this time I listened for a clunk. The second bin gifted me with the heavy sound I was looking for. When I opened it, I was in heaven. No computer, but there were no less than a dozen pairs of shoes. Jimmy Choo's, Prada, Coach, Chinese Laundry, even the pair of Toms I loved so much were in that box. I slid the old worn canvas shoes onto my feet and let out a sound of satisfaction. Nothing had felt this good in a long time.

I dug to the bottom to where my version of boots lay. Thigh-high with four-inch heels, the black boots had been a splurge even for me. Yes, $12,000 was a lot, but hand-tooled Italian leather was expensive. I lined up the shoes in front of the fireplace like trophies. It was so good to be reunited with old friends.

Set Up

Pepper stirred. He walked to the door and pawed it. "You're making this easy." I fluffed the top of his head, grabbed the leash, and took him outside. He piddled a bit, and we returned to the house. Once inside, I put a bowl of food down. He looked at it and walked back to the couch to lie down. The poor guy was exhausted.

One look at the clock, and I realized I'd spent too much time ogling my shoes. It was after six, and I was late. Pepper didn't budge, and I knew he'd want to stay asleep. He had hardly moved from that spot since we got home.

"Behave yourself," I said to the sleeping dog before I stepped out the door.

Chapter 13

ROLAND

Where in the hell was she? I arrived at six on the dot. The hamburgers and dogs were grilling, the beer was flowing, and she was nowhere in sight.

Despite the fact that I didn't want to attend, I couldn't stay away. After that kiss, she had me all twisted up inside. I popped the cap off a bottle of beer and took a long, slow draw. I had drunk too much at the bar last night, that was my excuse. Several beers and a shot wasn't a plan for good decision-making, especially when it came to curvy brunettes with lips like a porn star and a body to match.

"Thought you weren't coming." Keagan grabbed a cold one from the ice chest.

"Changed my mind."

"You changed your mind, or—" he tossed his head toward the first cabin "—she changed your mind?"

"You're too damn observant." I looked at the cabin and shook my head. "What in the hell is it about these girls?"

Keagan looked at his wife. "It's everything, man. They blow in here like a storm and whip you into shape." He didn't take his eyes off Holly. She was just starting to show her pregnancy.

"Does having a kid scare you?"

Set Up

"No." He sipped his beer and then laughed. "I'm a liar. It scares the shit out of me, but I look at her, and I know everything will be great. My child is growing inside her. Our lives are growing together."

I closed my eyes and imagined my future wife, and the only face I could summon was Natalie's. "You're a lucky man."

"Tell me that when my son is crying all night and those beautiful breasts of hers belong only to him."

"You're having a boy?" Jealousy gripped my chest. I wanted what everyone else had. I wanted someone to share my life with.

"I have no idea, but a man can dream. However, if a little Holly is born, I wouldn't be disappointed to have the two most beautiful women in the world belong to me."

"Here's the thing. I can't stand Natalie, and yet I can't stand to be away from her. I've got too much shit going on to let myself be distracted." I kicked at the dirt under my feet. "We have the breeding, I have clinic hours, and my damn office girl didn't show yesterday. I *really* don't have time for Natalie."

Keagan smiled around the lip of his bottle. "She needs a job."

"Oh, no. I'd never get a thing done with her there."

"Or…maybe you'd get a lot done." Keagan's eyes moved back to the cabin.

When I followed his line of sight, Natalie turned the corner and walked toward the group. Every time I looked at her, my heart took off like a wild stallion. Needing to observe the situation with less alcohol and more clarity, I slunk back into the shadows.

Natalie pulled up a chair next to Mickey. I couldn't hear a word they were saying, but Natalie talked with her hands, so I watched her gestures. Something was as tall as her hip. She rolled her eyes—a habit she had—and laughed loud enough for the sweet sound to cross the fire pit and grab me in the gut. She wrinkled her nose, pointed to her clothes, and started laughing again. By the sounds of Mickey's laughter, it must have been quite a story. Megan and Holly pulled up chairs near the blazing fire pit. Natalie's skin glowed under the flickering flames. I leaned against the big oak tree and watched.

Killian hooked up his Bose speakers, and Luke Bryan sang about stripping it down. Cole made his way to the pit and stood behind Natalie. His hands massaged her shoulders. I liked the man, but I didn't like his hands on my girl. *My girl?* When had I started thinking of her that way? Was it last night when I tasted her lips, or was it the minute she fell out of that damn truck? It took everything in me to stay put when I really wanted to wring that young man's neck.

The tree bark ate into my back, and I stepped forward. Natalie shrugged Cole's hands off her shoulders and stared at me. So many questions passed between us. Did we pretend the kiss didn't happen? Did we acknowledge it did? Did we move on, or did we move forward with whatever this was?

I tossed my empty beer bottle into the bin and pulled another from the cooler. Mickey stood up and whistled through her teeth. The damn sound was loud enough to get the attention of everyone three ranches over.

Natalie's eyes left mine and shot toward Mickey. Damn Mickey for breaking the only connection I had with Natalie.

"Thanks for coming over. Glad to see everyone here." She scanned the group, and we all moved closer like bugs to light. When had Toby and Tyson shown up? The damn woman sidetracked me. That's why I couldn't have Natalie in my life. I didn't pay attention to anything but her when she was around.

"The Junior Rodeo is right around the corner, and I wanted to say thanks for all your hard work. Natalie is coming on board to take over the books. This is a huge deal for me. But you are all making a huge contribution."

She looked around the area and connected with each of us. Mickey saw value in everyone's contribution, whether they were slinging manure or training livestock. "It's going to be great for the kids, and the ranch needs to be known for these types of goodwill projects. We're at full capacity for boarding, but I've put a hefty deposit down to have the stables expanded, doubling our capacity by summer. With the breeding services, boarding, and planned horse auction this summer, we need to expand. Take care of what we have because until the expansion is finished and we fill those stalls, money will be tight." Mickey raised her bottle. "Here's to the best crew in Colorado."

Toby called out, "So, I shouldn't ask for a raise?"

Mickey nodded. "You should be paying me to put up with your shit."

Toby raised his bottle to his lips. "Right on."

Cole cuffed him on the chin, sending him stumbling back. Everyone laughed.

Everyone filled their plates with hamburgers, hot dogs, and chips. I kept to the shadows while Natalie sat in the same chair and watched me. The conversations floated around like dust motes. One minute it was the weather, and the next it was rescues.

Kerrick stood on a chair and tapped his bottle with a knife. "One more announcement: Mickey has decided to make an honest man out of me. We've set the date for our wedding. A real cowboy affair right here on the ranch. Mark your calendars for June 18th."

The hoots and hollers were near deafening. Kerrick stepped down and walked to Natalie. His voice caught on the wind. "I checked it out, and it's registered to you." He handed her something, and pure relief flowed across her expression.

"Thanks so much." She hugged him—which, irrationally, I didn't like—then turned back to her friends.

The girls huddled together to congratulate Mickey while the men dug into the cooler for another bottle of beer.

"You're next." Killian nodded at me, then glanced toward Natalie.

"I don't see a ring on your finger." Killian was as good as married. We all knew it. Megan was wrapped around the man's heart like a relentless fist.

"It doesn't take a paper to know you're married in your heart. Megan is the only woman for me." Killian raised his beer in a toast. "Here's to ex-cons, and the men they allow to love them."

I considered the word 'ex-con' and thought about Natalie. "What was Natalie's crime?"

I kept hearing about theft of some sort, but it didn't make sense.

Natalie was an accountant. Was it white-collar crime? Embezzlement? She didn't come across as a criminal, but neither did any of the other women living on the ranch. They were normal people making a play for a normal life.

"You'll have to ask her. You know Mickey's rule." Killian, Kerrick, and Keagan sounded like a finely tuned trio. "It's her story to tell," they said in unison.

I glanced over my shoulder to the woman who was a mystery to me. I knew nothing about her, but I felt connected to her in a way I'd never experienced. As if she knew I was watching, her head turned my direction and she offered a weak smile.

I nodded toward her and turned to face the men. I had no idea how to handle this situation. Somehow, I'd reverted back to an eighteen-year-old boy asking a girl to prom. My stomach knotted. My neck ached with the need to turn and stare at her beautiful face. At thirty-two, wasn't I beyond sweaty palms and pounding hearts?

I broke into the men's conversation. "I'm going to check on the mares and then head home."

"We're going to Rick's," said Toby. "Care to join us?"

"I've had enough of Rick's."

I chugged the remainder of my beer and tossed the empty bottle into the trash bin, then I walked into the dark toward the barn. I would never be able to go to Rick's and not think about Natalie and that kiss. It took every bit of control for me not to turn around and look at her. My boots scraped along the gravel and echoed into the night.

Chapter 14

NATALIE

That damn man. He had kissed me like he owned me last night, and tonight he acted like we were strangers. I willed myself not to give a damn, but it didn't work. I gave a damn the second I fell out of the truck door and landed at his feet—the minute he touched my thigh and my heart at the same time.

The party was dying down when Roland disappeared into the darkness without so much as a hello or a goodbye. A light flickered to life and glowed in the distance.

Furious with him—but more so with myself for allowing him to toy with my emotions—I flew to my feet and knocked over my chair. The girls scrambled back like I'd spilled a drink on them.

"I need to talk to Roland."

I didn't wait for a response. They could think whatever they wanted. Maybe they could make more sense out of this situation than me. All I knew was, whatever burned between us was getting settled tonight.

I stomped across the dark field and into the barn. My initial response was to rage at him for ignoring me, but if I were honest with myself—and that seemed to be taking place more often lately

—I was hurt. I wasn't the kind of girl men overlooked, or at least I hadn't been years ago.

I lifted my shoulders to prep for battle and turned the corner into the stables. Roland stood with his back to me, petting the neck of the pregnant mare. He talked to her like she was his therapist.

"What am I going to do with that girl?" The horse swished her tail back and forth. "She's driving me crazy. One minute I want to kill her, and the next I want to kiss her. God, I want to kiss her. She's all wrong for me, and yet something feels right." He leaned his head against the horse's muzzle and groaned.

I crept deeper into the barn, sticking to the periphery. I should have felt guilty listening to his private confessions, but I didn't. My need to know more about Roland superseded my sense of right and wrong.

Surrounded by the smell of hay and his cologne—sandalwood, and sage—I felt at home, and the thought jarred me. I wasn't hay. I wasn't ranch. I was…what was I? I no longer had a clue.

His voice moved over me like a hot shower on a cold day. "What am I going to do with that girl?" Roland repeated.

Out of the shadows, I crept toward him. One step, then a second, and a third, until I stood at his back. "Kiss me." The words were freed before I could question the wisdom of letting them loose.

Roland spun around. I'd never felt so nervous in my life. Would he kiss me or walk away? It was a fifty-fifty shot at this point. He'd told the horse he wanted to kill me. Then he'd mentioned a kiss. Two powerful emotions—love and hate—separated by a thread. Which would he choose?

"How long have you been there?" He stepped forward and towered over me, sending my heart racing.

Eye level with the vein that pulsed in his neck, I reached out and picked a piece of hay from his collar.

"Long enough to hear the two options you're debating. I'd rather have you kiss me."

We stood toe to toe. "Natalie." He bent over and whispered in my ear, sending a thrill coursing across my skin. "This is going to end badly." His lips brushed along my neck. "I'm the nice guy.

You won't be satisfied with that for long." He stood back and looked down at me with those amazing eyes. They were a combination of colors that started as sapphire blue at the edge; in the center, little starbursts blended into the shades of sky and tropical water.

I reached up on my tiptoes and bit his bottom lip. "Don't fool yourself, you're not that nice." I sucked on the heated spot my teeth sank into seconds before. "Kiss me," I begged.

He threaded his fingers through my hair and covered my mouth with his. A fiery inferno of heat spread through my body. Every cell vibrated with want and need.

I climbed him like a tree until my legs wrapped around the trunk of his waist. He walked us to the wall and pressed me into the hard wood, but it wasn't that hardness I noticed as much as the stone-like erection pressed between my legs.

"What's going on with you and Cole?" He rocked my body against the wall, his hardness rubbing the exact place I needed him the most.

"Nothing. He's a friend, that's all."

We breathed in each other. Hard and fast, we rushed toward satisfaction. I moaned into his mouth, and he pulled away.

"I didn't like him touching you." His tone was forceful and possessive.

"Shut up and touch me."

"What are we, animals? I'm not taking you in the barn." He scanned the stalls around us. A dozen or so horses hung their heads over the rails, looking our way.

"Yes, we are." I pulled him back and sucked on his lower lip.

He released me, and I slid down the barn wall to my feet.

"No, we're not." Roland's chest rose and fell with each ragged breath.

"Are you going to leave me again?" I stepped back and crossed my chest with my arms. "That's so unfair, and it's so not nice."

"No, darlin', I'm not leaving. I believe you have a cabin. What if I show you how nice I can be?"

Thank goodness. I wasn't sure I could survive another rejection.

"Let's go." I grasped his hand in mine and took off toward my cabin before he changed his mind.

"Slow down."

"No." I yanked harder. "You aren't changing your mind."

He pulled back, and I came to a dead stop in front of him. "Natalie. I'm not changing my mind." He pulled me to his side and closed his arms around me.

Off to our right, Kerrick and Mickey banked the fire and watched our every move. They raised their beers in a salute.

"Hurry." I broke free and rushed ahead of him to my door. When I threw it open, everything changed. "What the hell?"

Roland walked in behind me. "What happened in here?"

"Pepper!" I yelled and stomped across the room, my foot sliding across a pile of poop. I looked down at my soiled shoe. "Pepper, how could you?" I hopped on one foot across the floor, which was now littered with the remnants of my chewed-up shoes. The dog hid in the corner, shaking.

The smell wafted to my nose and turned my stomach. Dry heaves doubled me over.

"When did you get a dog?" Roland pulled off my soiled shoe, walked it to the front door, and tossed it on the porch.

I hopped to the kitchen, kneeled over the trash can, and lost my dinner. While I retched, he cleaned. The man was a saint. On his knees with a bowl of soapy water, he scrubbed Pepper's gift from the carpet. I lay with my head on the cold tile floor next to a half-eaten bowl of kibble.

"Natalie, are you okay?" He dumped the dirty water into the sink, and I retched again.

"No."

He lifted me up and took me to the couch. "Lay down." I felt like the dog, with him as my master. Roland walked toward the black beast quivering in the corner.

"I thought he was such a good dog. I hate him. Look what he did!" I scanned the living room. There was one heel of a shoe left. The strap from the Jimmy Choos was chewed straight through, then

I saw the black thigh-high boots. I flew from the couch as if a snake had bitten me.

"You didn't."

Aghast, I raced toward the strip of soft leather lying next to the fireplace.

"Nat, you're scaring him. Stop yelling."

I raged on. "Stop yelling? You're telling me to stop yelling? The damn dog ate over $15,000 worth of shoes!"

I bent over and picked up the pieces—a heel—a strap—a buckle from the Prada slip-ons. I let out a growl that could scare a bear and stomped to my room where I slammed the door shut.

Several minutes later, a knock sounded. Roland didn't wait for permission to come in. He opened the door and entered.

"Pepper is really sorry, but this is your fault."

I sat up in bed and stared at the man in disbelief. "I didn't eat my shoes."

Roland approached and sat on the edge of the bed. "It is your fault." He reached up and pushed my sweat-drenched bangs from my forehead. "You left him alone."

"He was asleep." I scooted back and leaned against the wooden headboard. I wanted Roland in my bed, but this wasn't how I pictured it. "I fed him before I left. He didn't need to eat my shoes."

"First of all, you don't feed a dog and leave it. Food stimulates their bowels. They eat and poop. Second, your shoes are like crack to a dog. Rawhide in its finest form."

I started to cry again at the thought of those strips of chewed black leather. "I loved those shoes."

"Apparently, so did he." He crawled up beside me and pulled me against his chest. "Why a dog?"

"I wanted to make a difference in someone's life." Tears pooled in the corners of my eyes and ran down my cheeks. "You should have seen him. He was alone in that bleak cage. He'd given up. The lady said he'd made a mistake, and his family had turned their backs on him. I knew how that felt. Now I know why they got rid of him. You can't walk around town without shoes." I buried my head in Roland's chest and wept.

"He's a dog. He was only doing what dogs do."

"Yeah. They poop and eat your shoes." My sobs continued.

"Yes, they do that when left on their own. Pepper didn't know your expectations. He needs to be trained." His warm hand rubbed down my back.

"I told him to be good."

"You need to be trained, too."

I wiped the tears from my eyes. "And who's going to do that?"

He lifted my chin and looked into my eyes. "Me. Now go get a shower. You smell worse than your dog. I'm taking Pepper outside to show him the proper place to do his business, then I'm going to fix you something to eat." His eyes rolled down my body. "You eat like a bird, and you can't afford to miss a meal."

I *was* hungry. I nodded, rolled off the bed, and went straight to the bathroom. One sniff of myself, and my stomach heaved again.

Chapter 15

ROLAND

Joy. Passion. Disappointment. Resignation. Shock. Every emotion was pulsing through my veins. She was naked in the shower, and I was outside walking her four-legged surprise.

Pepper searched the grassy field next to her cabin until he found the perfect weed to water. The dog looked up to me for approval, and I ruffled his fur. "Good boy." His excited tail swung like a bullwhip whacking me across the shins. "You're not on my good side yet, buddy. I'm not fond of cockblockers."

As I closed the distance between the field and the house, I imagined Natalie in that moment. Her body would be pink and slick from the hot water dancing over her skin. No doubt her nipples would be hard and pebbled from the force of the jets.

God, she was a sexy woman. I was so close to getting to know her body until this beast of a dog intervened. Was it fate that kept us apart or fate that pulled us together? She was like a constantly rotating magnet, pulling me in and pushing me away.

Talk about strange. It was hard to believe this was happening. One minute I was drinking her out of my system, the next I was devouring her. I avoided her, only to almost take her in the stables with a handful of witnesses nearby. What the hell was she doing to me?

I preferred my women low-key and subtle, and there was nothing subtle about Natalie. She was a blinking neon sign that screamed needy, high maintenance, and trouble.

"Let's go." I tugged the leash and led the dog to the front door. Once inside, I went to work cleaning up the remainders of her shoes. "You had to eat one of each?" I hung the sexy untouched black boot in front of Pepper's face. "You have no idea what you sacrificed." The dog hung his head and walked into the corner like a three-year-old put in timeout. I raised a red stiletto and shook my head. "Dude, that was criminal." What I would have given to see Natalie in those with nothing but her bra and panties.

Just as the last shoe went into the trash bag, Natalie turned the corner. Her hair hung wet over her shoulders, dampening the thin material of her T-shirt. Yep, perky pink nipples showed through the thin white cotton of her shirt. My eyes ran the length of her body. Dressed in plaid flannel shorts, she was all legs and so damn hot.

She eyed the dog in the corner. Plump lips puckered into a frown, and all I wanted to do was press mine against hers to ease their tension. "You." She pointed at the dog. "You ruined everything tonight."

"Not everything." In two strides, I stood before her and cupped her face. My lips brushed against hers. This wasn't the hot, passionate kiss we shared earlier. This was more, and I realized right then I wanted more. A rushed roll in the sheets wouldn't be enough for me. I wasn't that guy.

She tasted like peppermint and smelled like fresh-squeezed orange juice. "Hungry?"

She rubbed her body against mine, causing my dick to twitch. "Mmm…hmm." Lips turned to tongues; tongues turned into hands that explored each other. Damn it. The woman was irresistible.

It took every ounce of self-control I possessed to break the kiss, but I did. "I'm talking about real food." I ran my fingers between the curves of her breasts and rested my palm on her flat stomach. "I like my women with curves." I moved my hands to her hips and squeezed. "You have amazing curves, Natalie. Let's keep them."

"I'm hungry for something different." She slid her hands up my chest and wrapped them around my neck.

"I'll feed all of your hunger in due time. Right now, I'm going to feed your stomach. Then we're going to get you on a plan to earn your dog's trust and loyalty." We looked at Pepper, whose head lay on his paws. He lifted it like he knew we were talking about him.

She glanced at the trash bag containing what Pepper considered chew toys. "I'm still mad at you," she told him.

"Why a dog? You don't seem like a dog person. Especially a big dog person."

She licked her lips and eyed the pathetic animal. "I've never had a dog, but I wanted one." She followed me into the kitchen.

"A cat would have been easier." I pulled out a chair and coaxed her to sit before I opened the refrigerator to take stock of what she had to offer.

"I suppose, but aren't dogs supposed to be man's best friend?"

I nodded while I pulled eggs, cheese, and ham from the refrigerator. "Why him? I would have pegged you for a designer dog kind of gal—one of those dogs that peeks its head out of your purse while you shop."

"Do you know how expensive those dogs are? I looked for one—it was $3,400, and she wasn't even the pick of the litter. Then I went to the pound, and they wanted over $400 for a dog that looked like a naked rat."

"How did you end up with a pit bull mix?"

Her eyes opened wide. "Pepper is a pit bull?"

"He's a mix. I'd say he's pit bull and black Lab. How do you not know this?"

She let out a groan. "I didn't pay attention. One look at him, and I knew he was like me. He'd made a mistake. He got caught. He did his time. I paroled him."

The frying pan hissed as I poured the egg mixture into it. "I'm proud of you, Natalie." Her expression brightened, and she sat up taller. How often had Natalie heard those words? Rarely, judging by her reaction.

"Let's see if you're proud of me when I take him back."

"You're not taking him back. He needs you."

"Yeah, well, I need him, too." Uncertainty flashed across her features. She stood and walked to my side. I flipped the egg mixture in the pan. "How do you do that?"

"It's all in the wrist." I demonstrated how I got the mixture moving back and forth in the pan, then gave it a little extra momentum to flip over and land back in the pan. "Want to try it?"

"No, I think I should start with something simple, like maybe boiling water." She pulled two plates from the cabinet and placed them on the counter. She and I worked side by side, and it felt right.

"I'm sure anything you cook is amazing." I slid the omelet onto a plate and turned off the burner.

"I don't cook."

"What do you mean? Everyone cooks something."

She grabbed the plate and walked to the table. "If you're not cooking one for yourself, then you have to share this with me." She cut a bite-sized piece and lifted it. Strings of cheese stretched from the plate to her fork. She twirled it around until the cheese gave up. "Mmm," she moaned the minute the food hit her tongue.

That sound she made sent a bolt of energy through my body. I'd re-create that sound, only next time I'd pull it from her lips while I tasted her.

"So, tell me about your specialty."

"Are we still talking cooking?" She raised her perfectly tweezed eyebrows.

"For now," I teased.

"You'd starve to death with me. My specialty is microwaving leftovers from whatever restaurant I had the night before."

"Now I have to help with your dog and teach you how to cook?"

"No, you have to help with my dog and cook if you ever want to eat." She swallowed the last bite and smiled.

"Are we negotiating the terms of our relationship?" I reached out and took her hands, elbowing her empty plate out of the way.

"Is this a relationship?" She pulled her lower lip between her teeth and bit down.

My tongue sought the spot on my lip where she bit earlier. "You have a thing for biting lips."

"I have a thing for your lips." She crawled into my lap and nibbled on my lower lip.

"Back to the negotiations. As for a relationship…I'd like to move in that direction. I don't do the one-and-done so popular these days."

She leaned back and narrowed her eyes. "I don't do long-term."

I craved the taste of her, so I buried my mouth in that tender space between the neck and shoulders and took in her shiver as it traveled up and down her body. "Why is that?"

She tilted her head and presented me with the other side of her neck. "No one can put up with me long enough."

Why in the hell would she say that? She was as cute as a marsupial. She smelled like oranges and tasted like rock candy. Who wouldn't want her?

I flicked my tongue out and traced her skin from her neck to her ear. "I like you, Natalie, and I'd like to try something more than a day with you." I didn't enter into a relationship thinking about the next one. One-night-stands left me feeling hollow. Hookups weren't my thing. I was done with meaningless sex. I needed something more.

"I'd like to try today with you." She shifted and straddled my lap.

"If I stay tonight, Natalie, I'll be here tomorrow."

She pressed her beautiful breasts against my chest. "You sound like a virus."

"What's it going to be, darlin'?"

"Stay with me," she whispered.

"You know what you're saying, right?"

She nodded. "I'm saying I want to be infected with your virus."

"I have to warn you, as far as viruses go, I'm the most virulent kind."

She squirmed against my hardened length. "God, I hope so."

Her ass fit perfectly in my hands. I gripped both cheeks and lifted her with ease. As we passed Pepper, I said, "Behave yourself."

Natalie laughed. "Like that will work." She buried her face into my neck. Her kisses stoked the fire burning inside me.

"It better because if he causes another stall in our plans, *I* may take him back to the pound myself." I walked into the first room on the right, flipped the light switch on, and kicked the door closed behind me. I lowered her with care onto the unmade bed. Her skin was flushed; her breath, uneven. She was a damn beautiful sight.

Chapter 16

NATALIE

I spread my arms across the bunched-up comforter. I should have made my bed, but I was on strike. Three years of folding hospital corners were enough for me. Besides, I wasn't expecting company.

"Sorry, the housekeeper didn't show up."

Suddenly, I was nervous. I pulled the collar of his shirt and tugged him toward me, hoping to shield myself with his body, but he held fast, perched above me, taking me in—staring—looking at me as if he really saw me. That scared the hell out of me. No one who really looked at me stayed long. I was used to get-in-and-get-out relationships. No one had expectations, no one left disappointed, and no one got hurt. But his words about long-term hit me in my heart. Could I be someone's long-term? Could I be his long-term? Something made me want to try.

His eyes deepened to sapphire as he raked them over my body. He licked his lips, as if tasting me there. I wore a T-shirt and flannel shorts, and yet I felt sexy under his gaze.

"What are you thinking?" Deep and throaty, his words flowed like hot syrup over my body.

"Too many things." I tugged at the hem of his shirt until I wrestled it up his torso. If I felt naked, he was going to be naked, too. He stood and pulled it off. *Holy hotness.* "Look at you." The man was ripped. Hills and valleys of muscle started at his neck and disappeared into his jeans.

He blushed all the way to his blond roots. "I'm not interested in looking at me." He pulled at the hem of my shirt, and in one movement it was gone, floating through the air to land on the clothes piled in the corner. "Look at *you.*" Roland didn't dive in like most guys. He absorbed everything with a look. "You're perfect." He straddled my legs, pinning me in place with the weight of his body.

"I'm not perfect." I brought my arms up to cover my chest, but he stopped me mid-movement.

"Don't hide from me. I want to see all of you."

He pressed my hands to my sides and ran his fingers up my stomach, making it flutter and quiver under his touch. My nipples tightened and pebbled as goose bumps covered every inch of me.

Soft and light, he drew circles on my skin from the elastic waist of my shorts to my collarbone. Around and around, he traced the swell of my breasts. I arched off the bed, trying to reach for his touch, offering him the places that craved it most.

He leaned forward and braced himself above me on his strong arms. He started his torturous assault to my body at my ears.

"Don't think, just feel."

A whimper left me. "Hurry up." It had been too long, and I was impatient.

His tongue traced down my neck and over my skin—hot and wet. He hovered over my nipple, the heat of his breath burning me from the outside in.

"I'm in no hurry. I've got all night." He latched onto the rock hard nub, and I came off the bed.

"Let's hurry." Each word was released on the exhale of a ragged breath. "We can take more time the second time." I wasn't above begging for what I needed, and I needed him inside me now. "Roland, please."

"I like that sound—you begging." He moved to the other nipple and gave it equal billing. He licked and laved and sucked until I was close to coming. Who knew that was even possible?

I fumbled with the button on his jeans. "Off. Take them off."

He gripped my hands and pulled them above my head. "I'm not rushing through this."

His sweet lips covered mine. Our tongues danced. His was soft and soothing. Mine was hard and demanding. We were always battling. From the minute I met him, he was like a burr in my sock. I was always aware of his presence. And even though he irritated the hell out of me, I couldn't shake him loose.

When he shifted down my body and gripped the waistband on my shorts, I sucked in a breath. Now we were getting somewhere. I rocked my hips, hoping to hurry the process along. He cleared my thighs, and I sang a silent hallelujah. My body shook like a caffeine junkie. Roland stopped at my knees and kissed my healing injuries. Frustration came forth in a growl.

"Impatient."

"Damn it, Roland, it's been a long time."

Once he divested me of my shorts, he crawled back up my body and shimmied his way between my thighs. This would have been perfect, except he was still in jeans.

"How long has it been?" Heavy-lidded, his eyes stared at me from under a fringe of bangs. He dipped down and heated my needy flesh with a stroke of his tongue.

"Too long."

"I heard rumors about you. Something about a little lady love." He pulled that little bundle of nerves into his mouth and sucked.

I rose up to my elbows. The sensation was like being electrocuted in a good way. "You're kidding me. They told you I had sex with Ryan Gosling?" I covered my face with my hands, hoping I could joke past this awkward moment. I couldn't believe my so-called friends were spreading truths about me.

He pulled them away. "We're in a relationship, Natalie. Don't you think I deserve the truth?"

"Will it make a difference?" I worried my lip.

"No, I just want to know who I'm up against." He leaned on his elbows, making himself comfortable between my thighs. "Ryan Gosling, huh?"

My voice withered. "When you close your eyes, you can imagine anyone."

A laugh rumbled through his chest. "Fair enough, but I have one rule, Natalie. When I'm between your legs, I want your eyes open and on me. I want to own each one of your orgasms. I'm not giving a single quiver up to Ryan Gosling. Understood?"

I nodded and fell into complete rapture when his tongue went back to work. He suckled, and licked, and nibbled every centimeter of my neediness. My body shook so hard, it probably registered an eight on the Richter scale, but I kept him in my sights. He never let up on me, and when two long fingers slid into my heat, I exploded. My lids grew heavy and fluttered closed.

"Open those eyes, Natalie. I own that one." As I caught my breath, he pulled his fingers out so he could strip down to nothing. He was long and lean. One solid, thick muscle bobbed between his legs.

"I haven't had one of those in a long time." I stared at him in awe. He was a masterpiece: long, thick, and hard for me.

"Do you still want me?" He tore the foil packet he retrieved from his wallet. "Make sure, Natalie, because I'm not the kind of guy who walks away." He stretched the latex over his length and positioned himself at my entrance.

Was he warning me or reassuring me? Didn't all men leave? At this point, it didn't matter. I wrapped my ankles around his ass and pulled him toward me. Tight didn't begin to describe the fit. I was like a damn virgin again.

He pushed forward and retreated until he was fully seated, and I was bursting. "So damn good," he groaned.

I felt whole for the first time. He had demanded I watch him and nothing else. This man who barely knew me wasn't taking anything from me. He was giving me himself. That was a new experience for me.

He rocked against me and built up sweet friction—the heat rising until I clawed at his back and begged him for release. "Not yet, sweetheart." He slowed the pace and brought me down, only to increase it and take me to the edge again.

"You're not nice!" I screamed at him.

"You keep telling me that."

His hips pistoned into me until I couldn't breathe. With a shift of position, he had me flying over the edge. His jaw tense and his teeth gritted, and he held his own release until mine was complete. Several thrusts later, he gave in to his pleasure. Because he demanded, I watched him. His chin tilted back, and his eyes looked skyward. His mouth…oh, his mouth softened into an O that let out the sweetest, most satisfied moan I'd ever heard come from a man. In that moment, I owned him.

All two hundred plus pounds of him covered me. Bumps rose on his back as I feathered my fingers across his skin. His warm breath tickled my neck. I giggled, breaking our post-coital bliss.

"That was amazing." He lifted himself from my body, and his absence weighed heavy on me. "Stay here," he said, his voice pitched low.

He walked out and minutes later returned with a glass of water and warm washcloth. With a gentleness that belied his bulk, he cleaned and cared for me, then climbed back into bed and pulled me against his chest.

"You still think I'm mean." Soft kisses floated over the top of my head.

"I like your kind of mean." Splayed across his chest, I breathed him in. He was fresh air, sunshine, sandalwood, and sage, and tonight he was mine.

"I love the way you smell."

"That's a start, but give it time; you'll hate me for something tomorrow. It seems to be how you and I get on."

"Oh, even when I hate you, I still want you." There was truth in my words. I rose up and expected to see the fear in his eyes, but it wasn't there. Wasn't this where he grabbed his pants and ran and I spent the rest of my night with a good bottle of red wine? Apparently not. Roland said he was staying, and he meant it. Imagine that.

"Glad to hear it." He rolled to his side and tucked me next to him. "What do you want to do tomorrow?"

"Tomorrow?" I hadn't thought of the reality of tomorrow. Sure, he said he'd be here, but so did a handful of other men who disappeared out the front door in the wee hours of the morning.

"Yes, Natalie, tomorrow."

I rolled over to face him. "I'm going to start on Mickey's books. She needs help, and I have the skills to do it. It's my way of contributing—making a difference." I twirled the hair on his chest and watched it spring back into place. I loved the feel of it against my face. He wasn't all furry and bearlike; he had just the right amount to be manly. "Then I'm scouring the paper for a job. I don't have a lot of cash, and my mom and I are at odds right now."

"About that…I have a proposition for you."

"Aren't you supposed to proposition me before you sleep with me?"

"Oh baby, we haven't slept yet." He pressed his burgeoning length into my stomach, and the tingles began anew.

I slipped my hand down to grip him. "Talk fast, lover, because you're right, we aren't finished."

I gripped and stroked while he attempted to string a sentence together. "I need office help, you need a job. It's perfect. You're hired. Start Monday."

He rolled away and grabbed his wallet for another condom.

"We haven't finished negotiating." I pulled the foil packet from his hands and ripped it open. "Are you paying me in dollars or inches?" I struggled to put the condom on him.

"Give me that." He rolled it on with ease. "If I was paying you by the inch, I'd have a major credit."

"Give me your best deal." I pushed him on his back and straddled his body.

"Fifteen dollars an hour, free pet training, and the use of my body without reservation."

He gripped my hips and nudged at my opening.

Fifteen dollars an hour? Never in my life had I worked for so little, but he was adding in pet training and his magnificent cock.

"Deal," I said and sank myself onto his length.

"Best damn negotiation ever."

He sounded pained as I rode him hard. This time, it was fast and fabulous. Sated and sweaty, we lay twined together like twisted licorice.

Just before I fell asleep, I realized I'd hit a trifecta. I had a dog, a real job with Roland, and a volunteer gig with Mickey. Surely, Mom couldn't deny me now.

Chapter 17

NATALIE

Reaching behind me, I searched for his body. I groped and grabbed across the bed, expecting to find a mass of hot, hard muscle. All night long, he'd nestled up to me. I was little spoon. He was big spoon. Now he was gone, and only an indent in the pillow remained.

Sore in all the right places, my body hummed with satisfaction, but my heart ached from loneliness. He said he wouldn't leave me, and yet he did. All men leave. They either die or sneak out of your bed in the morning. Why did I think he was different?

Flopped onto my back, I relived the night. We made love three times before I sank into a deep sleep. The soft mattress, cool sheets, and his arms wrapped around me lulled me into a blissful sleep.

Pepper barked, and I flew straight out of bed. I had a dog. *Shit.* Shit was something I didn't want to be greeted with this morning. I scouted out my pajamas in the corner, dressed, and ran for the living room.

Surprise and relief greeted me. Pepper sat at attention in the kitchen while Roland stood at the stove, cooking breakfast. His jeans hung low on his hips—his upper body bare. Each movement made the muscles of his broad back ripple.

"You're going to spoil me." I rushed behind him and slid my hands around his waist.

"Not possible." He flipped a pancake and placed it on a nearby plate that was six high. "You're already spoiled."

"Stop listening to the girls." My fingers skimmed over his chest, grazing the hardened nubs of his nipples. He sucked in a breath and hissed.

"I don't need to talk to the girls. Who owns a dozen pairs of shoes worth $15,000?"

I looked down at my penitent pooch. "Not me. Not anymore."

Roland turned around and kissed me. "Good morning, by the way." His lips lingered on mine for a lifetime.

"Morning breath." I stepped away and looked around for a cure. On the counter sat his coffee. After a big gulp and a couple of swishes, I deemed myself passable. "Better," I said and moved in for a proper kiss. "I thought you left." How much that had hurt me was a surprise. Maybe it was because I hadn't been alone in years and the thought of it bothered me.

No, that wasn't it. I liked the quiet of the past few days. I was hurt because he made a promise and I thought he broke it. But he didn't. He was in my kitchen, cooking me breakfast, and my dog was looking up at him like he was a god. After last night, I was in agreement.

"I said I'd be here." He took the plate of pancakes to the table. "Coffee?"

"That's one thing I can make for both of us." I headed to the pot. "Do you want a fresh cup?" He nodded, and I added my contribution to breakfast. Pepper eyed me with suspicion.

"He's been waiting for you."

"Right. I saw him pining at my door."

"He's a dog. Food always wins when it comes to canines." Roland forked a few pancakes onto two plates and plopped a dollop of butter on each pile. "Give him a pet."

While the last cup of coffee spit and sputtered to completion, I kneeled down in front of the big black beast. "Come here, boy," I called.

Pepper looked between me and Roland, then walked slowly in my direction. Another negotiation. This one, I wouldn't win with a smile or a swivel of my hips. I'd have to meet him in the middle.

My fingers reached for him and softly pet his broad forehead. He inched forward until my hand stroked the length of him. "No more shoes, okay?" He followed me to the table, where he lay across my feet.

Roland liked his coffee black, whereas I needed cream and sugar. I'd always said I wasn't sweet enough on my own and needed help.

"Tell me about yourself, Natalie."

"I can't cook." I looked down at the pancakes in front of me. "I had this in my cupboard?"

"You had the ingredients. I threw the stuff together, and presto, we have pancakes."

I drizzled syrup over the stack. "You're amazing."

He smiled the kind of smile that could make a girl wet. "You told me that a lot last night. I'm glad you still think so."

Heat flushed to my cheeks. "Last night was amazing."

"Yes, it was. Now stop deflecting and tell me about yourself."

"Myself? You screwed me stupid last night, and I don't even know your full name." Not odd, really, but this was supposed to be different.

"Roland Mallory." He reached over and pushed my bangs to the side. "No hiding either."

"Lord, you're persistent."

"Lord, you're stubborn. Now spill."

I blew out a frustrated breath. "What if you don't like me after you know me?"

His eyes softened. "Natalie, I already like you. That's not going to change."

Trust didn't come easy for me. Daddy said he'd be home Thursday, and he never showed up. My life was never the same.

It took three deep breaths to begin.

"Natalie Diamond here."

I pointed to myself and shared my story—just the past few

years. He didn't need to know that as a child I had a stuffed monkey named Bo Bo, or that I wore braces from age twelve to fourteen.

His fingers brushed across the watch. "You went to jail for this?"

"Sounds silly now, but in hindsight, it was about more than the watch."

Funny how talking about stuff often made it clear. I loved this watch, but not because it was a Cartier. I loved it because it was my grandmother's, and she told me she loved me enough to give me her proud possession. That was a lie, too.

"It was about a broken promise."

"And yet you still wear it."

"Can you believe my cousin Rachel took it off and left it on the counter of the employee bathroom? She never understood the importance of this watch. A promise was made to me, and I made sure it was kept. I was tired of empty promises. I figured if she didn't want it, then I'd take it, so I did, and I got caught."

I circled the face with my fingertip. "I sacrificed a lot for this, and I'll never give it up. Grandma was always there for me, especially after my father died. And then gradually she disappeared. She had left in mind before she left in body. Alzheimer's is a cruel disease."

He pushed his empty plate away and placed mine front and center. He cut a bite and fed it to me. "I get it. Promises are important. Integrity is important. Tell the truth. Be yourself. Own your mistakes. You've owned yours."

"What about you? What's important to you?"

Roland cut another bite and placed it in my mouth. "My father built the vet clinic on his good reputation. I've followed in his footsteps. My dad's a nice guy."

I swallowed. "Too bad you didn't inherit that trait." I stuck my tongue out like a child.

"You're going to see how nice I am soon enough." The legs of his chair screeched across the tile floor as he pushed back. Poor Pepper flew to his feet and ran into the living room.

"Promise?"

"Come here." He pulled me into his lap.

"I never say anything that's not true. My entire life is built on the cornerstone of my reputation."

"It's a good thing we aren't banking anything based on mine."

"You're a little tarnished, but we can shine you up." He nibbled on my neck. "Let's start here."

And he did. We started on the kitchen table and finished in the shower. This man was going to kill me, but I'd die a happy woman.

AN HOUR LATER, Pepper and I were on our own. Roland took off for his house to get a change of clothes and pick up things for my dog. Dating a vet was going to be a boon after all.

He left me with strict instructions to walk Pepper every couple of hours and not let him out of my sight. He put him on a feeding schedule, which Roland promised would get him on a pooping schedule.

On his leash, we walked around the ranch. Pepper backed away from the horses, but that made sense—to a dog, they must have looked like a bigger dog.

If it weren't for Pepper, I would have taken the brunt of a thousand jokes about Roland. Except for a few pointed remarks about my overnight guest, everyone paid attention to the dog instead, which was a relief. I didn't know how to explain what Roland and I were doing together. I didn't understand it myself.

After the rounds, we knocked on Mickey's door. She opened it with a devilish smile. "I want details." She pulled me inside and slammed the door shut.

She appeared to be alone. "Where's Kerrick?"

"He got a call early this morning."

"Does that happen all the time?"

"As long as there's crime, there are calls."

She walked deeper into the house and led me to a back room outfitted into an office. The place was dark all over. Dark wood. Dark walls. Poor lighting.

"No wonder you don't get anything done. A morgue has more light."

She skipped over to the desk lamp and flipped it on. "It's an Ott lamp." It glowed to life and lit up the room like sunshine.

"Still, this place is gloomy."

She lifted her shoulders. "It was my dad's office, and I can't bear to change it just yet. How's the beast?" She looked down at Pepper, who was sitting next to me.

"Short of chewing up all my shoes and shitting on the carpet—which Roland cleaned—he's great. Actually, he's a very sweet dog."

"I still can't believe you of all people got a dog, and a mutt at that." Her eyes left the dog and focused on a nearby bookshelf. She pulled a shoebox of receipts from the shelf and opened a ledger. "This is what I have. It's all on the computer. I can give you access and a password if you have your own computer; otherwise, you'll have to work here."

"I'll work here until I figure it out."

"Did you unpack?"

"Just my shoes and underwear, and you see how well that went for me. If it weren't for Roland, Pepper here would have been back in his cage at the pound."

"That would be downright mean."

"It's not off the table yet. We have to see how we adjust to each other."

"Speaking of we, how did you and Roland turn into a couple?" She pointed to the desk chair and took a seat on the foldout next to it.

I slumped into the old leather chair and wheeled it close to the desk. "I wouldn't call us a couple just yet."

"Roland is not the kind of guy you mess with, Natalie. Don't hurt him. I love him like a brother."

"Let me tell you that man is no nice guy, and I wouldn't want him as a brother."

"Why?"

"He's too damn good in bed. What I did with him, I could never do with a brother." I fanned my face with a page from her ledger.

"He's not a one-night guy."

I held back a laugh. "No, he's an all-night guy. And a next-morning guy."

"Oh, wow. Now I don't know if I want the details."

"You don't." I shuffled through the pile. She had numbers all over the place. "Your books are a mess."

"I know. You think I invited you here because I liked you?" She pulled me over and rubbed my head with her fist. "I needed an accountant."

I pushed away and sat up. "I understand about negotiations. I scored a job at Roland's clinic, free pet training, and the use of his body."

"What did he get?"

"Me."

"He's way too nice and a shit negotiator." She gave me an I'm-joking smile, but somewhere in her words, the truth resonated with me. I was no prize.

"You know, I tried to set him up with Holly and Megan. I wouldn't have guessed it would be you, but I'm happy."

What the hell was it about me that made normal things seem impossible? "He's been with Holly and Megan?" Jealousy snaked through my body.

"No. I tried to set them up, but the girls weren't interested. They went McKinley all the way."

Relief swept over me like a cooling current. I loved Holly and Megan, but if they'd been with my man, heads were going to roll.

My man?

"Good. I'm not a sharer."

"Yeah, sharing isn't one of my strong suits either. I'll leave you to this mess. Let me know if you need anything."

Three hours later, I was finished reorganizing her receipts. They were all listed in the wrong categories. It was a wonder the ranch was in the black. When I walked into the living room, Mickey was gone. No doubt taking care of her horses. I looked at my watch for the thousandth time today. When would Roland be back? What if he never came back? That was silly; he worked at the ranch, and of

Set Up

course he'd be back. I reasoned with myself for minutes and gave up.

"Ready to go?" Pepper jumped to his feet and wagged his whip-like tail.

It was close to feeding time, so I took him home and poured a bowl of kibble. He gobbled it right up. Five minutes later, I got the leash. "Potty time." I checked my back pocket for the plastic bag I shoved in there earlier. When would they make a breed that didn't poop?

Sure enough, ten minutes into our walk, Pepper left his gift in the tall grass. With my arm stretched out as far as it would go, I picked it up in the bag and gagged until my eyes watered. But hey, at least it wasn't on my carpet.

Chapter 18

NATALIE

"Look at you. You're turning into a responsible pet owner. I'm proud of you."

Roland stood next to my cabin dressed in blue jeans and a button-down shirt, looking sexier than he had a right to, as I trudged back with Pepper and his gift.

"This is the worst." I held the bag out to my side and turned my nose in the other direction.

"He's a good dog, Natalie. Be grateful pooping is the worst thing he does."

"Don't forget he ate my shoes." I tossed the bag into a nearby trash can and tugged at Pepper, who was sniffing at a prairie dog hole.

"Speaking of your shoes." Roland held out a box. "I tried to save your old ones, but I couldn't. I hope these will work for you."

I ran to the man bearing presents. "You got me shoes?" That was as good as foreplay in my book.

"No, these are from Pepper."

I traded Roland the leash for the box. Inside were the exact Toms I had yesterday, only these were new. "You really are a nice guy." I gripped his collar and pulled him down so I could kiss him.

Set Up

"I think you have a little nice in you, too." He wrapped one arm around me and pulled me to his side. "If you don't have dinner plans, I picked up Chinese takeout. We could do a normal couple thing like watch a movie."

"We're a couple?" These were odd concepts to me. Hell, Debra Watson, aka Ryan Gosling, was my longest anything, and that only happened because we were imprisoned together for years. "I'm honestly surprised you came back."

"Get in the house, Natalie. We're getting ready for another fight, and I don't want it to be public." Up ahead were Holly and Keagan and several of the ranch hands. Their curious eyes were on us.

"I'm not fighting with you. I've started to really like you."

He walked a few steps ahead to his car, reached in, and pulled out several bags. "Glad to hear it. Now go on in."

Stunned, I stood still and watched Pepper and Roland pass me and walk into my house. I trailed behind them by a few feet, the scent of fried rice guiding me inside.

I set his gift on the coffee table and met him in the kitchen. "Why do you want to fight?"

"I don't. I'd rather be snuggled up next to your quivering body, but that's not happening until you get it in your head that I'm a keeper. I don't want you wondering each time I leave if I'm coming back. I'm coming back, Natalie, unless you tell me not to."

"I'm sorry. This is tough for me. Three years ago, I had a life different from the one I have now."

"Tell me about your life, Natalie. Who didn't come back for you? Who wounded you so much that you can't trust me?"

My heart beat like a tribal drum. My lip quivered as I tried to suppress the tears. For the past seventeen years, I'd deflected similar questions.

Why do you shut me out?
You end everything before it begins.
Tell me who hurt you.

I never felt compelled to tell anyone until this man. "My father."

He gripped my shoulders and hugged me. His scent was like Xanax to my senses. He calmed me. "What happened?"

"It's a long story. Let's get our food, and I'll be our movie." I couldn't believe I was going to share this with him, but then again, he had bought me shoes.

Curled up in the corner of the couch with a plate full of orange chicken and fried rice, I began.

"Seventeen years ago, on August 13th, my father left to go on a hike, and he never returned." I put a bite of the sweet chicken into my mouth to counteract the bitter taste of disappointment. "A year later, he was declared dead." I shook my head and raised my hands. "He was here, and then he was gone. He promised he'd be home in a week. He promised, Roland."

Roland put his plate down and moved in closer to me. "I'm sure he tried."

"He did. He was my everything. Mom was always busy. The money in my family came from Dad's side, but Mom ran the business for him. Talk about a silver spoon—he was born with one in his mouth, and she had one stuck in her ass."

"I'm sure she's not that bad." The pads of his fingers brushed gently over my tucked up legs.

"She is who she is. I'm who I am because of her." I reached for my glass of water but couldn't quite grasp it. Roland handed it to me. "Dad was the mom. He took me for ice cream, walked me to school, braided my hair. He loved me."

"I'm sorry, baby."

No tears were shed until he called me 'baby'. Dad had called me that all the time. "Dad died, and all the warmth was replaced by stuff. My mother filled my sorrow with places and things. I'm hollow, Roland. I'm an empty vessel. My only value is my value—my trust fund—and I don't even have that now. I've known my worth all my life, and so have the people around me."

"Bullshit. You're full of it." He pulled my plate from my hands and set it on the table. "Look at me."

I raised my eyes to look at him. "Repeat after me. I am worthy of love."

I shook my head. "Not even my own mother wants anything to do with me."

"Say it," he rumbled.

I rolled my eyes and gave him what he wanted. "I am worthy of love."

"Good, because Natalie, I can't fall in love with someone and not have them return my love. If you can't love yourself, you can't love anyone else. Now, repeat after me. I have value beyond my bank account."

"I have value beyond my bank account." I swiped at the wetness on my cheek.

"I am a good person."

I repeated phrase after phrase until he was finished trying to convince me of my worth.

"I want to make love to my boyfriend." He smiled like a player.

I smiled at his sneakiness. "I do." And we did. Right there on the couch. We couldn't leave Pepper alone with our dinner. He couldn't be trusted.

ROLAND CHOWED down on cold Chinese food while I flipped through the channels. "When are you going to unpack?" he asked.

"I am unpacking. I'm taking the less-is-more approach."

"Natalie, less is just less. Seeing these sitting here makes me feel like you have one foot in and one foot out the door."

The truth was I did. I had no intention of staying in this cabin long term. "I'll get to it."

He tossed his plate to the table. The silverware clanked across the wooden surface. "You're not planning on staying here, are you?" It wasn't a question, but a statement of fact.

I looked around the room. "I'm not really a ranch girl."

"I can't believe it, Natalie. Were you planning on sharing that with me, or were you going to thrust your greatest fear on me? I'd show up with beef and broccoli, and you'd be gone?"

"No, just because I don't live here, doesn't mean anything. I'm getting my inheritance soon, and I plan on buying a place of my own. We can be there together."

He eyed me with skepticism. "Right."

"What do you mean, 'right'?" All the air was sucked from my chest.

"Nothing, it's just—I don't know you any other way than who you are in this cabin."

"I'm the same girl." Was that a lie? When I had my millions, would I be happy to sit on the couch and eat Chinese food? "We'll still have our love-hate relationship. Half the time, you want to throttle me."

He broke a smile. "That's part of your allure."

"I promise there will always be a part of me you want to murder, but having just spent three years in prison, I wouldn't recommend it. No Chinese food." I picked at my cold orange chicken, glad we'd just hurdled over another crisis.

Not long after that, Roland kissed me goodnight and left me alone. Was he pulling back to protect his heart? I'd tried to convince him things wouldn't change, but it was hard to do when I couldn't convince myself.

He left me directions to the clinic and asked me to be there by nine. I kissed him at the front door and felt an ache in my heart when he drove away. I didn't deserve him, but I wanted to.

A few minutes after I climbed into bed, the mattress shifted and Pepper snuggled up to me. Roland recommended I kennel him at night, but there was no way I'd lock this dog up again.

He pushed his body next to mine and let out a long sigh. I rolled over and wrapped my arms around him. This was going to be a very different night than the last one. Instead of long hours making love with an incredible man, I would be sleeping next to a heated fur ball who had the breath of a skunk. I loved it less, but I loved it anyway.

Chapter 19

NATALIE

Pepper and I showed up for duty at ten minutes to nine. I was young when my dad disappeared, but there were tidbits of him that stayed with me. He often shuffled me out of the house, saying, *Early is on time, on time is late. Let's go, Natalie.*

Roland opened the door and let me into the lobby of his office, where the walls were filled with pictures of pets and the air smelled like antiseptic. He leaned in and kissed my cheek. "I missed you."

"You could have stayed."

"I had to go." His eyes were soft and sad.

Behind us, the bell on the door rang and Roland stepped back. "Hi, Mrs. Clarkson, how's Bubble?"

An old woman somewhere between seventy and a casket entered the lobby with her arms filled with a cat. What could have been a dozen cats was actually one—a jumbo cat? Bubble seemed a fitting name.

Pepper growled, and I tugged on his leash. "Let's get you checked in, okay? My name is Natalie, and I'm Dr. Mallory's new assistant." I walked behind the desk and tied Pepper to the leg of the chair. Roland came up behind me. His hand touched my hip when he leaned over me to switch on the computer. It was a little touch, but it meant so much.

Up popped his calendar for the day. Mickey could learn a thing or two from Roland about organization.

He pointed to the screen, which showed Bubbles' treatment plan—shots and deworming. It sounded awful. I nodded my head. "I got this."

"Thanks, Natalie." His hand slid from my hip across my back, keeping contact until his fingers dropped from the distance he put between us.

He ushered Mrs. Clark into the back room while I became acquainted with his setup. The bell above the door rang again. A young man walked in and propped a small cage on the counter. Inside was a rodent. I cranked my head back and looked at the computer screen.

"You must be Luke, and this is Mike?" I took a closer look at what the schedule called a sugar glider.

"That's us."

"Dr. Mallory will be with you in a moment." Several minutes later, Bubble and her owner were approaching my desk.

"How did it go?"

The woman smiled so wide, her cheeks rounded like apples. "Oh, that Dr. Mallory is a good one." She sighed the way a teenage girl did when she saw her crush.

"That, he is." I looked over my shoulder at the man who made my blood boil, for good and for bad. "That will be $65."

Mrs. Clarkson didn't blink an eye. I could have charged her double, and she would have paid.

The bell jingled again. Pepper stood up and inspected the guest. Cats were not his favorite, but he certainly showed interest in the little yellow Lab that trotted in.

A bit later, Luke came out with Mike. "How'd it go?"

He laughed. "Turns out Mike is actually Michelle, and we're pregnant."

"Oh, my. Should we celebrate or…"

The young man nodded his head. "It's all good."

Set Up

"Whew. I'm so glad." He paid his bill and was on his way. The rest of the morning flew by with birds, cats, and a rat with a bad tooth.

"Time for lunch." Roland pulled off the white coat that had 'Dr. Mallory' embroidered on the pocket.

"Shall I get you something?" I jumped from my seat and nearly tripped over the dog.

"Careful there. I have a supply of Band-Aids, but I'd hate to see your pretty skin marred again."

"Still thinking I'm pretty, huh?" I was fishing, but after last night, doubt and vulnerability had taken up residence.

"You're beautiful. That won't ever change. Hungry?"

"Starving," I cooed.

"For food, Natalie." He untied the leash and walked Pepper out the front door.

I jogged to catch up. "That's what I was talking about."

He chuckled, low and throaty. "Yeah, right."

I looked behind us at the door. "Are you going to lock the door?"

He lifted the keys and pressed a button. A *beep beep*, and it was done.

"Where are we going?"

He lifted his head toward the corner where a bunch of trucks sat in a row. "Best place in town." Pepper sniffed the air and picked up the pace.

"Food trucks?" This was another first. A diner was a stretch for me, but a rolling roach trap was entirely different. "This is frightening."

"Trust me." He threaded his fingers through mine and pulled me along. The crazy thing was, I did trust him, with everything.

After eating two pork tamales drowned in green chili, we made our way back to the clinic. People were already waiting outside.

"You're busy."

"I am. I've reduced my days at the clinic down to three a week so I can help with the breeding and semen samples at the ranch. I also volunteer my services for the animal rescue when I'm needed."

"So you need me, then."

I was teasing, but the solemn look he gave me took my breath away. "More than you know, Natalie."

The rest of the day was a blur. Two kittens, a pug, and a dachshund later, we were finally done.

Alone with Roland in the office, I powered down the computer and turned toward him. "Will you come over? I'll fix you dinner."

He lifted his brow in disbelief. "You're going to fix me dinner?"

I laughed. "What I mean is, I'll run by someplace and pick up dinner."

The war within him was apparent in his eyes. "I've got a few things to take care of." He picked up my wrist and looked at my watch. "I'll stop by around seven. Will that be good?"

"Perfect." Actually, right now would be perfect, but I couldn't complain. Roland was coming over, and I was excited.

"Feed him and walk him when you get home." He brushed a kiss across my lips and walked me to the door. It *beep-beeped* as soon as it shut.

I LIFTED and shook each of the blue bins. Any that made a swishy sound were moved to my bedroom. My best guess was they contained clothes. The rest were stacked in the corner. At least it looked like I was making progress.

Stripped out of the black slacks and shirt I wore to the office, I now wore a sundress I never would have bought on my own, but I liked it. On my feet were my brand new Toms. I could have unpacked those bins in the closet and found something fabulous to wear, but this outfit felt authentic for the ranch, and I was trying my best to embrace that feeling.

The crunch of his tires on the gravel signaled his arrival. "Pepper, he's here."

We stood at the door, both wagging our tails. Behind me, the tiny little table was set like a five-star restaurant with folded napkins and wine glasses. The aroma of stuffed manicotti filled the air.

Long legs unfolded from the driver's seat. In his hand were flowers. *He brought me flowers.* I melted.

"Hey," I stepped off the front porch and ran to him.

"Oomph." The air whooshed from his lungs as I plowed into him.

"I missed you." I jumped up and wrapped my legs around his waist, and he wrapped his arms around mine.

"It's been two hours."

"Two hours too long." Those two hours felt like a lifetime. Roland had worked his way into my system like the virus I accused him of being. I peppered his neck with kisses. "Are you hungry?"

"Starved." His voiced vibrated from deep in his chest.

"For food, silly."

"Of course." He balanced me with one hand and handed me the flowers with the other. "For you."

"Aww, I love them." I smelled the mixed bouquet. It had been at least a decade since anyone bought me flowers.

"Are you going to be bearing gifts every time you come?" I slid from his waist to my new Toms shoes.

"Will that make you happy?"

"You make me happy."

He grabbed a bottle of wine from the front seat. "How's our boy?"

Our boy? That sounded so sweet and permanent.

"He's fat and content." Pepper sat on the porch, waiting for our return. "Whoever gave him up was stupid."

Roland closed the door. His lips whispered against my ear. "Whoever gave you up was stupid."

I smiled so wide, my jaw hurt. "Yes, they were. Their loss is your gain. Now come inside. You owe me kisses. Do you have any idea how hard it was to be with you all day and not kiss you?" I rushed inside with him on my heels.

"I was trying to be professional. How would it look if I was pulling my assistant into the back room at every turn?"

I hung my head and puckered my lips in a pout. "I want to see the back room." I led him into the kitchen and pulled out a chair. "Have a seat."

"You made me dinner?"

"'Made' is a broad term, as you know, when it comes to me and cooking." I pulled the foil trays from the oven and served them up on the white plates I found in the cupboard. "I also bought wine." I held up the expensive bottle I couldn't afford but bought anyway. It had been sitting open on the counter, waiting for his arrival.

"You have exquisite taste." He poured the blood red liquid into the waiting wineglasses and handed me a glass.

Smooth and fruity, the wine danced across my taste buds. "Let's eat!" I was in a hurry to get this prerequisite over because once we ate, it was time for dessert, and I was craving Roland.

After dinner, we moved to the living room. He looked at the boxes in the corner. "Looks like you unpacked some."

"I shifted stuff around a bit." It wasn't a lie. I did shift four boxes into my closet.

"That makes me happy."

I climbed into his lap. "I could make you happier." And I did. All night long.

Chapter 20

NATALIE

Roland kissed me goodbye before he left for work. He said something about house calls and he'd see me later in the day. Clingy and needy had never been my style, but every minute I spent with Roland made me want another. He really was like a virus, but a good virus that infected the best parts of me. He made me want things I never knew I wanted.

"Must be nine o'clock," I said to Pepper when the pounding began. "Let's go." I rolled out of bed and into some sweatpants and a T-shirt. I really needed to unpack my boxes. Three years ago, I never would have been caught dead in something so common; now, it hardly seemed to matter. I would never fully accept the idea that clothes were just clothes, but on the ranch they didn't matter all that much.

When I opened the door to take the dog outside, I was slapped in the face by cold air. The wind whipped around, and a few flecks of snow started to fall. Spring storms were common in the Rockies. Some of the worst storms hit just before summer.

I wrapped my arms around my body and shivered while I waited for Pepper to find the perfect place. His ears perked up, and he bolted after a rabbit. His leash ripped from my hands, and he was free.

"Pepper, stop!" I yelled. I chased after the damn dog all the way to the staff stables.

Cole stepped in front of Pepper and brought him to a dead stop. "Whoa. You need to keep him on a leash. He could start a stampede."

I marched over and swiped Pepper's leash up from the ground. "He is on a leash." I shook the blue material in front of me. "He got away."

"Yep, so did you. I knew I should have put a leash on you, too." Cole shook his head and shrugged. "So, it's Roland?"

Oh lord, what was I supposed to say to that? The old me would have said something flirty, giving him the idea there was a chance for him and me. Hell, there would have been a chance. I could have moved my way through this whole ranch without giving it a second thought. Now I was different. I liked waking up to Roland. I liked hearing him tell me I was beautiful because he made me believe it.

"Yes, it's definitely Roland."

"You could do worse." Cole leaned over and petted Pepper. "He's a nice guy."

Last week that statement was the kiss of death for a man, and today it was a banner of truth. "Yes, he is a really nice guy."

"You win some, and you lose some." His eyes shifted to my T-shirt, and I realized it was way too cold for it to be appropriate standing out here in next to nothing.

The heat of embarrassment rushed over me. "I gotta go." I crossed my arms and pulled on Pepper's leash. "Bad dog." Already, I'd formed a habit of reprimanding him when the blame should've fallen on me. Like now—what the hell had I been thinking, going outside my cabin dressed like this? I had a boyfriend, for goodness' sake! The thought stopped me in my tracks: *I have a boyfriend.* I hadn't been able to say that for eight years.

After a breakfast of yogurt and fruit, I stared at the boxes in the corner. They reminded me of a hot burner on a stove. If I touched

Set Up

them, they were bound to cause me pain, but they were equally dangerous if left untended.

    I pulled the first one to the couch and slipped off the lid. This was the box that fell from the car that first day. In it was a lifetime of pictures. They had been boxed up for longer than I could remember. I ran my fingers over Daddy's picture. It was Halloween, and he was dressed as Disney's Beast. Of course, I was Beauty. There was one of Mom sitting behind her desk, sporting her classic Chanel power suit. A silver frame held Grandma's picture. She used to sit at the helm of Diamond Financial Services. That was before her mind started to slip.

    I looked down at the watch and remembered the last day she told me it would be mine. We were enjoying tea in her Capitol Hill home. She tapped the face of the watch and said, "Don't you just love a good diamond?" I wasn't sure whether she was talking about the watch or one of us. "This is one of my favorite things. I bought it when we went public with our stock." She sipped her English breakfast tea and continued. "The world, like this watch, can belong to you, Natalie. It's all yours. Find out what you want, and go after it."

    I had always thought she meant the watch was mine, but maybe she didn't. Maybe she was referring to opportunities. It didn't matter now; it was on my wrist, where it was going to stay. I loved how this watch represented the power of women and what they could do in business. It represented Sunday tea with a woman I admired and loved. This watch gave me value beyond its price tag because the woman who wore it had valued spending time with me.

    "What do you think, Pepper? Should we decorate?"

    I pulled more pictures from the bins. Some made me laugh, and some made me cry. I lined the fireplace mantel with representations of my past. My favorite was of me and Dad fishing. On close inspection, I was holding a worm. When had that little girl disappeared? The answer was simple. She disappeared the day her father did. He had been the one constant that kept her grounded and normal.

At the bottom of the box was Bo Bo the sock monkey. Pepper raised his head with interest.

"No, you don't. This is mine."

I hugged the lanky stuffed toy Dad won at the fair tossing rings over bottles. It was given a place of honor up front and center between the pictures. Pepper looked at it and lowered his head. We had an agreement.

The next box wasn't too bad. It held my computer, which buzzed to life when I plugged it in. Near the bottom of the container was a bunch of books on fashion, a stack of Elle magazines, and a goal sheet. I pulled it out and placed it on the table.

1. Never get a wrinkle.
2. Never wear polyester.
3. Never buy generic.

My expectations were low and shallow. The list shamed me with its lack of substance. At least getting my inheritance was a worthier goal than the ones listed here.

In the kitchen, I grabbed a soda and a pen and sat back on the couch in front of the list. I drew a line through number one and wrote, "Age gracefully." After crossing out number two, I replaced it with "Wear what fits the moment." In place of number three I wrote, "Be a good steward of my money." Whether dirt poor like today or wealthy beyond my dreams, I needed to use my money wisely. I didn't like feeling bankrupt.

A soft knock sounded at the door. I looked at my watch. The morning had slipped away from me.

I expected to see Mickey standing there when I opened the door, but it was Roland who stood in front of me. His bright smile lit up my day.

"Oh my goodness, you're here!" I pulled him inside and shut the door.

"Natalie," he warned.

"No, I wasn't thinking you wouldn't come. I knew you would come. I just didn't think it was you now." I ran my hands through my hair and dipped my head down to look at the sweatpants I still wore. "Oh, I look awful."

"You look beautiful." He held up a white bag. "I brought brunch."

"Oh, wow, you cooked for me."

"Yes, I went to a Natalie Diamond culinary class."

He was dressed in khakis and a button-down polo—a real frat boy look. "What did you bring us?" I led him to the coffee table and pushed away the papers in our way.

"Roach coach, of course."

I bounced up and down on the couch like a kid who was promised candy. "What is it? What is it?"

He sat beside me and tore open the bag. The smell of cilantro filled the air. The warmth of his body next to mine filled my heart.

"Lupe's famous carne asada breakfast burritos." He said it like he'd brought Beluga white caviar, only this was better than any fish egg.

"You're the best." I pulled a foil wrapper from the bag and dug in. Yogurt didn't hold me over for long. I was getting far too much exercise at night to live on minimal calories.

"So my diabolical plan is working?" He brought a steaming burrito to his mouth.

"What's your plan?" I wiped the grease that dripped to my chin.

"I thought I'd start with amazing sex, add in flowers and food, and you'd give me a few more days."

"Don't forget, you did give me a job."

"Yes, there is that. Speaking of which, how long do you think you'll want to keep that job?"

I shimmied closer to him. "How long are you going to ply me with sex, food, and flowers?"

"I don't have an end date in mind."

"Neither do I." I liked working at the vet clinic. I felt like I contributed something positive while I was there. "Are you ever going to take me to your house?"

"You've been there."

"I have not." I rose up and crawled into his lap, one of my two favorite places. The other was naked under his body.

"I have a studio apartment in the back of the clinic. It's not much, but it works for now."

"How did you end up living behind the clinic?" I would have expected him, as a vet, to have a big house. Surely, vets made money.

"It's economical. I bought the clinic from my dad and have been making double payments to get it paid off."

"Where's your dad?"

"Last week, my parents were in Maine. Once he retired, they sold the house and bought an RV, and they've been on the road since."

My eyes squinted, and my nose scrunched. "I don't think I could live in a rolling house."

He crumpled up his foil and tossed it on the coffee table. "It's not for everyone, but I can see the benefits of living in tight quarters." His hands flattened on my thighs and smoothed their way to my hips. His touch had a way of making me feel completely alive—an uncanny ability to bring out feelings in me I never thought possible.

"Maybe you're right. You've been living in my tight quarters for the past couple of days, and I've liked that."

He leaned forward and rested his head on my chest. "I like your tight quarters. I could live there forever." His lips brushed over the pucker of my nipple, and I shuddered.

"How much time do you have?"

"Not as much as I'd need to do everything I want." He bit at the tightened nub. "I really should get back to work."

"But you're not going to, are you?" I scooted in closer and rubbed against his hardness.

"You're making it hard."

Back and forth I rocked. "Yes, I am."

"You are so bad for me."

Warm hands slipped past the elastic waistband and gripped my bottom.

"Yes, but it's so good."

"It's the best."

"Roland, what if I never want to give you up?" It's funny how an internal thought can become words without the intention to set them free. I didn't mean to ask the question out loud.

"Natalie, I have no intention of letting you give me up." His face softened with sincerity.

This isn't a man just trying to get into my pants. He's been there many times, and he keeps coming back. Obviously, he's a masochist.

"Why?"

"Why what?"

His hands against my skin were a distraction. My chest rose and fell with each pass of his fingers over my hipbones.

"Why me? I'm everything you're not. I'm selfish. I'm spoiled. I'm empty."

Making quick work of pulling down his pants and putting on a condom, he pressed my sweats past my hips and impaled me with his hardness. "You're no longer empty, Natalie. I will fill you with everything you need."

When we connected like this, nothing else existed. "You deserve more than me." The truth was a hard lump in my throat, but it softened with every tender stroke. "You said you didn't want a project and—"

He silenced me with a kiss. "You're a challenge, Natalie. What man doesn't love a challenge?"

My need for him grew stronger each moment we spent together. I loved how he made my body feel, but more importantly, I loved how he made my heart feel.

"I'm needy." I pounded into him, trying to reach that moment of completion where I fell off the cliff and he was there to catch me.

"I can do needy." He gripped my hips and thrust deep inside me.

"You *are* doing needy," I said through gulps of air.

"I love needy." Our pace was frantic, both of us reaching for the same thing—a connection—a conclusion.

"You love me?" *Shit.* Another burst of unfiltered words rushed from my lips.

"I think I could, Natalie. I really think I could." He buried himself as deep as possible, and we were two bodies fused into one.

My heart and core exploded at once. I screamed out his name and flew over the edge, taking him with me.

I stayed there, draped across his chest and breathed in his essence and words. *He could love me.* Years ago, I would have run far and fast from those words. Maybe it wasn't that people couldn't stand me so much as their interest in something more scared me. To open your heart to love meant to open it to pain. Being loved by Roland would be worth the risk.

"I could put up with you."

He tickled my sides. "Put up with me? All I get is your tolerance?" I squirmed in his lap, and he slipped from inside me.

"What more do you want?"

He lifted me from his lap and set me on my feet. "So much more, Natalie. I want it all." He reached to the table for the tissue box and stopped when he saw my goal sheet. "What's this?"

I pulled up my sweats, took a seat beside him and pointed to the crossed out list. "Those were my old goals."

He cleaned up and put himself back together. "Those aren't goals. 'Never' is never the way to start a goal."

"I know." I pointed to the margins. "I revised it."

He looked it over. "These are your goals?" Creased forehead, narrowed eyes, pursed lipped—his expression was just like Dad's when he was disappointed.

"No, I was only updating the goals I made years ago. What are your goals?"

He sat for a thoughtful moment. "I want people to know me as a good and honest man. At the end of the day, my reputation is all I have to leave behind."

"A goal is not a goal unless you can measure it." That's what Mom said anyway. "How do you measure your reputation?"

"That's easy. It's measured by the people who think I'm special enough to give me their time, their talent, and their love."

I leaned into him and took it all in. "You're too good for me."

"We're good for each other." He brushed his lips across mine.

Set Up

"What's your number one goal?" He looked at me the way Pepper did when he wanted a treat.

"I want my inheritance." There it was, out in the open. At this moment in time it was my focus, because once I had that, everything would fall into place.

Roland deflated like a balloon. "So money is more important than anything?"

"It's important to me."

He looked down at my watch and back at me. "Someday you'll figure it out, Natalie."

I backed away from him. "Figure what out?"

"That money will never fill the void in your heart. Life isn't about money or things; it's about relationships. I thought we were on the same page. We're not." He kissed my forehead. "I'll see you tomorrow at the clinic." He turned and walked toward the door.

"Wait, you're not coming back? You said you'd always come back. Don't give up on me."

Roland turned around and wrapped his arms around me. "I told you I'd always be here. I want you, Natalie, but I want to be wanted, too."

"You're punishing me because I want my inheritance. It's owed to me."

"No, I'm not punishing you. I care about you. Maybe too much." He brushed my bangs to the side. "I've put a lot of things on the back burner lately. I let my attraction to you become a distraction. There are things that need my attention. Tonight is my catch-up night."

"I'm a distraction. That's what you're saying?" My throat burned and tightened. "A minute ago you were saying you could love me, and now you're telling me you can't give me top billing?"

He pinched his lower lip between his thumb and finger. "What I'm saying is, I care about you more than I should, and it's unexplainable because you and I are so different. If your top goal is to get your inheritance, you're telling me you love money more than you could ever love me, or anything else for that matter. I'm not sure I'm willing to live with that."

He turned and walked away from me. This wasn't anything like before. Our fights were always as volatile as our lovemaking. This was different. Roland was throwing down the gauntlet. I needed to figure out my priorities, and he had better be at the top.

"That's not fair."

He looked over his shoulder. "Life rarely is, but when you invest yourself in the important things, it's worth it." He reached for the doorknob. "Will you be there tomorrow?"

I opened my mouth to say yes, but only a squeak came out, so I nodded and he closed the door behind him.

I had never felt so alone in my life.

Chapter 21

ROLAND

Walking away from her was the hardest thing for me to do. I suffered from a savior complex that never worked out. I couldn't save Natalie; she had to save herself if there was any hope of us being together.

My boots kicked up dust on the way to the stables. Like the cloud of dirt that followed me, I felt heavy and depressed. When Natalie said her inheritance was the most important thing to her, my heart fractured a little.

That was my problem. I fell too easy and too fast. And if I didn't put the brakes on with Natalie, I was on a collision course with disaster. I'd not only lose her, there also was a real possibility of losing myself in the process.

Mickey raced to catch up with me. "You look glum." Side by side, we walked to the stables.

I heaved out a sigh. "Not a great day."

"Natalie?"

"Yep."

"You want to talk about it?" Mickey and I were like siblings, and if there was anyone I could talk to, it would be her—but to talk to Mickey felt like a betrayal of Natalie.

"Not really." Once in the barn, I made my way to a horse at the end of the stalls. Mickey had emailed this morning to let me know it was lame. "Was he shoed recently?"

"Yes, but I checked it out, and he seemed fine; no stray nails, no close clipping." She opened the gate, and we walked in. He was definitely favoring the right front leg.

I lifted it for a closer inspection. "He's bruised and should be fine in a few days."

"I'd say the same for you." Mickey patted me on the back.

"I really like her, Mick. She's so wrong for me, but it all feels so right."

"She's bruised, too. Only her bruises are deep. She isn't used to people loving her. She's used to people loving what she can give them."

"I'm not asking for anything." I followed Mickey out of the stall.

"I know you, Roland. You're asking for everything. Don't give up on her."

"I'm not. I'm just stepping back a bit. Giving her room to think."

"Do I need to go and see her?" Mickey looked toward the stable exit.

"I'm sure she could use a friend about now."

"What about you?" We walked outside and headed toward my truck, which just happened to be parked in front of Natalie's cabin.

"I could use a nap." I was worn through and through. Falling for Natalie was exhausting, but nothing worth having was ever easy.

"Go get your nap. I'll take care of our girl." Mickey kept walking when we reached my truck.

When she lifted her hand to knock, I drove away. Maybe gaining some distance would allow me to gain perspective.

Chapter 22

NATALIE

For a good twenty minutes, I blubbered and cried. Poor Pepper didn't know what to do with me, so he laid his head in my lap and whined along with me. What a pair we were.

When the knock sounded at the door, I ran to open it. It had to be Roland. Who made love to their girlfriend, only to leave her feeling like it was the last time? He promised he wouldn't leave me, then he walked out on me. Maybe he was back.

Roland wasn't there when the door swung wide. It was Mickey. She walked inside and pulled me into her arms. "Tell me everything."

I fell into a fit of tears that streamed endlessly down my face. Years of anguish poured out of me. Stupid stuff like when Mom forgot my dance recital and I looked out into the audience to find Rosa saving a seat that would remain empty the whole night.

Seventeen years of sorrow emptied from my soul, bringing me to this moment. Somehow we had moved from the hallway into the living room, where I lay on the couch with my head in her lap. She stroked my hair and told me everything would be okay, but I wasn't sure. I wasn't sure about anything anymore.

"I thought he liked me." My voice caught on every word.

"He does."

"He left me after we made love. Accused me of loving money more than I could love him." I began blubbering again, and Mickey handed me the box of tissues. "Did he tell you?"

"No, Roland is loyal to a fault. He only said you might need a friend right about now."

Mickey slipped from beneath me and walked into the kitchen. The coffee pot hummed and started spitting liquid. She was back in two minutes.

"Sit up." She handed me a mug as soon as I was upright. "What's this?" She pointed to the damn paper that started it all.

"It's nothing." I picked up the page and crumpled it into a ball.

"It's something. Tell me." She leaned back, lifted her boots to the table, and brought her mug to her lips.

"We got into a discussion about goals, and when pressed, I told him my goal was to get my inheritance." Mickey groaned. "What? It's owed to me." I seemed to be saying that a lot. The message was like a broken record on repeat.

"So you listed that as your number one goal?"

"Yes."

"What if Roland listed a bunch of things before you?"

"He did. He said his reputation was everything. I asked him to define how he measured it." I played back the conversation in my head. *It's measured by the people who think I'm special enough to give me their time, their talent, and their love.* "Oh hell, he was telling me he measured his worth by how people treated him, and I didn't put him on the top of my list."

"And you wonder why he left?"

I was an awful person. This man was opening his heart to me, and I'd told him my bank account was more important. In that moment, I knew without a doubt it wasn't true. He was right—I'd had money all my life, and I was never as happy as I was the past few days.

"Holly accused me of being a six-year-old. I think she's right. I feel like a kid in a woman's body."

"You are." She shifted so she faced me. "I'm not going to tell

Set Up

you to forget your inheritance. That would make me a hypocrite. We all have this ranch because I fought for what belonged to me. You keep fighting. You'll win, or you won't. The money will be there, or it won't. At the end of the day, it doesn't matter because if you don't have anyone to share it with, there's no point in having it. You can live without money, but you can't live without love." She leaned forward and put her empty mug on the table. "You of all people should know that. How much love have you received lately from the people who are supposed to love you the most?"

I was still on the "you can live without money" part when her next sentence bulldozed me over. I didn't know how to love because it had been so long since I was loved.

"I don't know how to fix this." I set the mug on the table next to Mickey's and buried my face in my hands.

"Yes, you do."

Mickey didn't elaborate. She simply lifted herself off the couch and left. That was Mickey's way, to leave you with a lot to consider.

I had no idea how to fix this with Roland. Maybe the solution wasn't there. Maybe the solutions lay inside of me. I needed new goals.

I got dressed and took Pepper for a walk. When I came back, I unpacked the rest of my stuff, but this time I looked at it like an outsider. Besides the pictures, there was nothing in those boxes that had value. I had ten designer purses but nowhere to wear them. I had a closet full of clothes that didn't seem to blend with the girl who walked out of prison. I hung up a pair of pants and looked at the inscription on the wall: *Life isn't about finding yourself. Life is about creating yourself.* Who did I want to be? Someone different.

At the kitchen table, I sat in front of a blank piece of paper and wrote out new goals.

1. Be worthy of Roland's love.
2. Be the type of woman, Mickey, Holly, Megan, and Robyn would be proud to call their friend.
3. Contribute to others so they feel loved.
4. Provide a good life for Pepper.
5. Prove to my mother I'm worth her love, not her money.

I sat back and looked at the list. Not one thing on it was self-serving. Everything was about someone else, and that filled me with pride.

The next thing I did was pull a cookbook from the kitchen shelf. How hard could cooking be anyway? I'd failed at boiling an egg, but nothing was riding on that egg. Today I was properly motivated. Tomorrow I would bring Roland a home-cooked meal. There was a fifty percent chance I would kill him, but I was willing to make the sacrifice as long as I made the point. Roland was worth any change I had to make—even if that meant learning how to cook.

PEPPER and I arrived our normal ten minutes early and rang the bell. Roland showed up with wet hair and a clean-shaven face. He smelled like home.

"Morning, Boss." I stepped inside and walked past him. What I really wanted to do was crawl up his body and ask him to hold me, but that wouldn't have been fair. I needed to give more to Roland than I took.

"What do you have there?" His eyes shifted to my hands, which held a casserole dish. The cookbook had said it was a simple recipe, and I had the ingredients. I was pretty sure the bottom wasn't supposed to be black, but hopefully, we could salvage enough for a meal.

"I made us lunch."

His brows lifted. "What place gives you their glass dishes?"

"No one. I actually cooked us lunch. I'm assuming you have a microwave in that studio of yours?"

He smiled his beautiful smile. "You cooked for me?"

I shook my head. "I cooked for us." I loved the sound of that. 'Us' had a nice ring to it. "Where shall I put it?"

"Follow me."

"Oh goody, I get to see your space."

I couldn't wait to see where Roland spent his private time. He led me through the back offices and straight into his one-room

Set Up

studio. That's exactly what it was; one room, unless you counted the bathroom, then it was two. On one side of the room was a full-sized bed, and on the other side was a kitchenette. In the center was his living area, equipped with a man-sized TV, a couch, and a La-Z-Boy recliner. It had everything he needed—everything but me.

I made room for the glass dish in the refrigerator and looked at the coffee pot on the counter. "Can I make a cup?"

The poor man was studying me like I was a different species, and in some ways I was. The old Natalie Diamond had died a painful death last night, and the new Natalie Diamond had risen from the ashes.

"Sure, help yourself." He opened the cabinet to show me where he kept the pods.

"Can I make you one, too?"

"That would be great. I take it—" He walked to the kitchen chair and picked up his white lab coat.

"Strong and bitter like, your women. I got it. Go take care of what you need. I'll take care of you."

He stood for a moment and stared. "Natalie, I owe you—"

"Nothing. You owe me nothing, now get. Mrs. Trent will be showing up soon for Buddy's shots. I'll bring your coffee out as soon as it's ready."

The bell on the door rang, and I hurried to get it. "Let's go, Pepper. We've got people to serve." The dog trotted behind me and walked to his place by my chair. I had started to love that dog.

"Good morning, Mrs. Trent. I'm Natalie, Doctor Mallory's assistant." I liked the sound of that. Assistant implied a partnership—a co-op of sorts—and if there was anyone I wanted to be paired with, it was Roland Mallory.

Once Buddy and his owner were shown to the exam room, I rushed back to finish Roland's coffee. The rest of the morning, I served Roland the only way I knew how—by serving his clients.

When lunchtime rolled around, I had already snuck back into his space and warmed up the casserole. Despite its less than appealing appearance, it did smell good. How bad could I mess up hamburger meat, cheese, and pasta?

Turns out, pretty bad, but Roland filled his plate twice. That was blossoming love.

"You're a glutton for punishment."

"No, it's good." He pushed the hard black piece to the side.

I laughed. "What makes it good?"

"You did. You went out of your comfort zone to show me you cared. That's huge." He pulled my chair over so it sat in front of him. "Natalie, I'm sorry."

I placed a finger over his lips. "Shh, I'm not." I shifted from my chair into his lap and replaced my finger with my mouth. God, I missed his kisses. It had only been a day, but I needed him like I needed my next breath.

"I'll cook *you* dinner tonight."

"Are you afraid two meals from me might kill you?"

He looked down at the blackened dish and smiled. "No, I was looking for a reason to come over."

"You're always welcome to come over."

"About that. Everything with us happened so fast. Do you think we should start from the beginning and get to know each other better? Maybe move a little slower?" He bit his lower lip.

I couldn't read him. I wasn't sure whether that was something he wanted, or needed, or thought I needed. "That's like trying to unlearn how to ride a bike."

"Natalie, I just don't want you to think it's all about the sex."

I cupped his face with my hands. "Roland, the sex is the best thing I have to offer you. Let's not throw that away."

He released a heavy sigh. "That's not true, but thank God I don't have to give that part of you up." He covered my mouth with his and kissed me until my toes curled. I was so caught up in the kiss, I didn't hear the bell ring, but Pepper did. He barked and danced around us until we paid attention to him. Yep, I loved that dog.

Chapter 23

NATALIE

Monday and Wednesday, I worked at the vet clinic. Tuesday and Thursday, I worked on Mickey's books. Friday, I split my day between the two. One Friday, Roland kept Pepper while I came back to the ranch to finish the week with Mickey. We were becoming a real family unit.

"Can you make the deposit?" Mickey asked. Boarding fees had flowed in all week. A small fortune waited to go into the bank, and since Mickey's account was barely flush, she needed the money available to pay upcoming bills.

"No problem. I'll be heading in that direction anyway." I turned off her computer and gathered up my things. "Roland and I are going on our first real date." Excitement bubbled inside of me and slipped out with a giggle.

"You sound happy." Mickey led me into the living room, probably so she could analyze my expressions. She couldn't see my face in the low light of the dark paneled office.

"I am. It's funny because my life is so different. I have a boyfriend, a dog, and a life on this ranch. Three years ago, that would have been the equivalent of moving to a third world country and contracting dengue fever."

"Three years in prison can give a girl a new perspective."

I contemplated that for a moment. The years in the cell were long, but I hadn't learned much in prison except new ways to get what I wanted. The real changes started the day I landed on this ranch.

"I've never been so poor and yet felt so rich. I'm wearing a dress that's four years old tonight, and I don't care. Roland will love it."

Mickey smiled up at me. "I think you may be growing up."

Her words ran through me like a hug that squeezed me from the inside out. "I think you may be right."

"Have you talked to your mom?"

And there went the warm, fuzzy feeling. An icy chill skirted across my body at the mention of my mother.

"No. I'm afraid to call her. Basically, she booted me out and told me to figure my life out."

"You really need to clear things up with her. Unlike the rest of us, you still have a mother. Do something with that relationship."

I shrugged. "There's nothing there."

"What about your inheritance?"

"I'm still working on it."

She walked me to the door. "I'm proud you're starting to embrace what's important, but don't forget your family is important, too." She pulled her phone from her back pocket and tossed it to me. "Call your mom."

I caught the phone and nodded. It had been two weeks since I'd had any contact with Mom. It wasn't like she had a way to get a hold of me, so I definitely needed to reach out to her. The problem was, I wasn't sure I was ready. "Are you trying to ruin my night?"

"No, just call her and toss my phone in the mailbox on your way out. Don't forget the deposit." She brushed past me, walked out the door, and turned toward the stables.

I stared at her phone all the way to my cabin. Calling Mom was like picking at a scab. Her complete disinterest in me was a wound that had yet to heal—and how could it, since it was constantly reopened?

Everything I did brought her voice into my head. All the things that disappointed her ran through my brain and ended with, *You're just like your father.* That was the best thing she ever said to me. Being like my father made me proud, but it also came to make me sad because over the years I'd lost a lot of my father and adopted the behaviors of my mother.

Diamond Financial belonged to his mother, who had passed it down to her daughter and my mother—not her son. Had my father ever felt jilted because his mother chose the business first? Maybe that was why he spent so much time telling me how much I mattered.

I slid a soft yellow dress over my head and put on my favorite pair of shoes. The Toms weren't the most glamorous, but they were important to me. I'd seen Roland's finances, and although he was safely in the black, he didn't have a lot of extra cash to buy things, so showing up with flowers or a pair of shoes meant he'd sacrificed something for me.

As I readied myself for my date, I kept staring at the phone. Mickey was right. Mom was the only family I had left, and I needed to mend the fences…or at least try.

I plopped on my bed and held the phone for a minute, as if waiting would somehow give me the courage to dial her number.

Oh, hell. I punched in the numbers and waited for her to pick up.

"Hello, Diamond residence," Rosa answered.

"Rosa, it's me, Natalie."

"Oh, Natalie. How are you?" There was a hint of excitement in her voice. It filled my empty spaces with hope.

"I'm really good. I've survived. I have a dog, a place to live, and a part-time job, plus a volunteer gig. I'm dating a nice man."

"That's super! What are you doing for a job?"

"I'm working at a vet clinic for Roland. He's the man I'm seeing." I didn't want to tell her too much about him. Lord knows he'd never get the seal of approval from Mom.

"Natalie, never mix business with pleasure." Behind her voice, I could hear some shuffling—which could only mean Rosa was taking notes.

"Are you writing this down for Mom?" Agitation colored my

voice. "You don't have to tell her everything, Rosa. I'll tell her myself. Put her on the phone."

Rosa let out a frustrated sigh. "She's not here. She left the day after you did. She's at the London branch."

I soaked in the silence around me. I'd just come home, and she had already left. No big surprise. How was I supposed to mend fences that stood taller than the prison gates?

"Why does she hate me so much?"

"She loves you in the best way she knows how."

"She sucks at love."

"Yes, sweetie, she does, but she excels at business. Your father was the opposite, and that's why they made a perfect couple. They compensated for each other."

I couldn't imagine my parents being attracted to each other. It was like mating a mongoose with a snake. "I'm making a difference in people's lives, Rosa, and I wanted her to know that. Write that down."

I wasn't sure whether I wanted to scream or cry. It's funny how when you're away from someone, you can create an entirely new scenario in your mind. I fantasized about lunches and dinners with Mom. Of course, there was a shopping trip or two in my illusions as well. Now the reality was setting in, and I realized I'd never even had those things. I wanted them, but they never came to pass. After Dad's death, Mom didn't raise me; Rosa did. It hadn't been part of her official job, but she'd stepped up and had done the best she could.

"I'll let her know. Oh, before I forget, your mom said to get your number if you called and tell you she'd meet with you a week from Friday at the house to discuss your progress."

I bit my cheek, trying to feel anything but anger. Even the pain of my teeth breaking the skin was less than my mother's disregard.

"I don't have a phone. This is a friend's number. I can't afford a phone."

"How does that feel?"

"Not having a phone, or not having the money to get a phone?"

"What feels worse?"

"Neither. What hurts is not having anyone who cares if I call. I've got to go."

"I care, Natalie." Her voice was soft and warm.

"After Dad, you were the only one who did."

"Shall I tell your mother you'll see her a week from next Friday?"

"Tell her what you want."

I hung up the phone and tossed it on my bed. I waited for the tears to come, but they didn't. I had nothing left to give that woman. From this point forward, I would love her, but my time would be spent with those who returned my love.

I shook off the bad feelings and covered my sadness with foundation, mascara, and blush. Roland and I were going on our first date, and it would be amazing. I gathered my purse and a change of clothes. I skipped like a kid to the car. Nothing would tarnish this night.

Chapter 24

NATALIE

Roland stood in front of Antonio's Italian Restaurant, looking sexier than he had a right to. Dressed in black jeans and a button-down shirt, he turned the head of every woman who walked past him. How could he not notice the women who ate him alive with their eyes? He didn't notice because he was waiting for me—with more flowers. How was it possible I had caught the eye of Roland Mallory?

He had me pegged from the beginning. He'd said I was spoiled and self-indulgent, and that was the truth. I was certainly that girl two weeks ago, but I'd changed. He'd changed me. When I fell asleep in his arms each night, I didn't need couture and riches; all I needed was Roland.

I stepped out of the car, and his eyes lit up. In several long strides, he was in front of me. "You look beautiful." He handed me the flowers. With the amount of blooms I had in my home, anyone visiting would think one of two things: I either had the nicest boyfriend in the world, or someone had recently died.

When his lips touched mine, I melted into his body. His kisses were like an opiate. The more he gave, the more I wanted. We stood outside, locked together for minutes. It had only been a few hours

Set Up

since I'd seen him, but I missed him. He had become an important part of my life. An integral part of everything that was good.

"You look beautiful, too." I threaded my fingers through his and walked toward the restaurant. "Aren't you glad I'm not cooking tonight?" The man was a saint. He'd choked down every meal I made this week without complaint. It was one more thing to add to my list of post-incarceration accomplishments. I had a pet, I'd found a job, and I hadn't killed him with my cooking —yet.

He stopped in front of the door and cupped my cheeks in his palms. "I'm happy to go home." He drew his eyes up in a questioning, sexy smirk. "You can boil me eggs wearing just an apron."

"Keep wanting, buddy." There was no way I was getting my fleshy bits close to heat and fire. It was bad enough I'd already burned my fingers a few times. There was no way I was bending over a hot stove and risking something more delicate. "We're having Italian, then I'm having you." I tugged him through the door.

A large group of people I recognized stood to the right as we entered. I stiffened and grabbed hold of Roland's arm, pulling it tight to my chest.

"You okay?" he asked.

Trying to avoid the crowd, I pressed my face into his shirt and inhaled his scent. Several breaths later, I nodded. "Fine."

"Natalie? Is that you?" a shrill voice called from across the room. The *click-clack* of heels on tile drowned out my groan. Victoria Kincaid was the original mean girl, and back in high school, I'd been her second in command. I was more ashamed of my association with her than going to jail.

A chill shook my body, and Roland wrapped his arms around me, offering comfort.

Time to blend in. I stood tall and pasted a Ms. Congeniality smile on my face. "Hello, Victoria." I leaned forward and air-kissed her cheeks.

"It's been so long," she said.

I was no shrinking violet, but her presence caused me to curl up inside.

Roland stood behind me and rubbed his palms up and down my arms.

"Yes, it's been a while." My words were delivered with sweetness, but there was a razor edge to my tone. She was a black cloud hovering over my sunny day.

"Where have you been?" She smirked at me and crossed her arms. It was her classic spill-the-beans look.

Her question was like a splinter just under the surface of my skin. She knew exactly where I was, but where had she been? Where had my so-called best friend been while I was stuck in the slammer for years?

"In prison." I said it loud enough for the group looking over my shoulder to hear. Victoria was the puppet master, and they were her toys.

"Oh, that's right. Now it makes sense why you're wearing that old dress. Don't you remember? I was with you when you bought it." Judging by the smile that ate up her face, Victoria was pleased with her insult. She looked past me to Roland. "Who's this? Your parole officer?"

Heat spread from my chest, up my neck, and to my cheeks. The angry burn inside was trying to find a way to escape.

"No, this is—" Roland stepped to my side.

"I'm Roland, Natalie's boyfriend." He claimed me with obvious pride. I leaned into his side.

Victoria offered her hand to him, but he ignored the gesture. He completely dismissed her, and my heart leapt with joy.

"What do you do, Roland?" Her eyes roamed over his body, and I wanted to claw them out. However, being the good chameleon I was, I continued to smile.

"He's a ve—"

"I'm a proctologist."

I whipped my head in his direction and stared into his mischievous eyes. He smiled the same condescending smile Victoria gave me earlier, but this was leveled at her. He leaned into me and whispered in my ear, "Let me handle this."

Victoria leaned in closer to Roland. "Oh, my. That's quite a specialty." It was obvious the mention of a doctor—no matter his field—was like crack to her, and she was drawn to her fix.

Roland cleared his throat. "Yes, proctology deals with assholes." His tone was even and professional. "And my particular specialty is helping bitches like you pull their heads out of their assholes."

The whole group gasped. And true to form, Victoria blurted out the cliché: "I've never—"

Roland piped in, "But you should have. You could probably use regular exams. It's unhealthy to keep your head lodged so far up your ass." He looked behind her at the men and women smirking. "Or theirs."

"Mallory?" the maître-d' called.

"Let's go, beautiful." His eyes danced with humor. "Have I told you how much I love that dress?"

As soon as we were seated, I placed the bouquet on the table, then I cupped his cheeks and drew his face to mine. "That was amazing. Do you have any idea who that girl is?"

"Yes, she's Victoria Kincaid." He pressed his warm lips to mine. "She means nothing to me."

"That's *the* Victoria Kincaid. Her father practically built Denver."

"He may have succeeded in building a city, but he failed at raising a daughter."

I lowered my head in shame. "She was my best friend all through high school and college." How many times had I acted deplorably to establish my place in her hierarchy?

"Thank God you went to prison and found some real friends." He waved over the waiter and ordered wine.

"What made you do that?"

He'd basically handed Victoria her ass. No one I knew would have had the courage to do that in private, let alone in public. Forget what I'd said about shoes—*this* was truly the best foreplay ever.

He turned in the booth and looked at me like he was looking into my soul. I felt warm and naked under his gaze.

"I care about you, Natalie."

My lip popped from between my teeth as soon as I smiled. "I

could love you, Roland." I slapped my hand over my mouth, appalled to have let my truth slip out. It was too soon, and a declaration of that magnitude was sure to send him running. "I'm sorry. I didn't mean to say that."

"No?" He slid my hair through his fingers and pushed it from my face. "I won't let you hide behind that beautiful chestnut mane of yours."

"I'm not hiding."

"You are. You're hiding from powerful emotions." He thumbed my chin and held me in place. "Are you saying you don't already love me?"

I closed my eyes and let his question caress my skin. I'd basically admitted it, so why shouldn't I own it? My voice shook as I spoke. "Love never works out for me."

"It seems to be working out now." His lips grazed mine just enough to start a fire in my body. "Are you happy, Natalie?"

"Mickey asked me that earlier."

"And?" He nuzzled my neck, nipping at the soft skin just below my collarbone.

"You're distracting me."

"No, darlin', *you're* distracting me." His hand dropped beneath the table, and his fingers slid up my bare thigh. "You've been addling me since you fell out of that damn truck."

My breath caught in my throat. The man was driving me crazy. Something had to be done, or I'd be lying in this booth with his hands up my dress.

"What did you do this afternoon?" I loved the way he talked about his on-call jobs and hoped he'd stop torturing me with his talented fingers and talk about his day.

"I checked out Tom Morrow's herd today. He lives on the ranch next to Mickey's."

The waiter brought the wine. Roland's hand came from beneath the table to hold his glass, and I rethought my decision to change the subject. I missed his intimate touch.

"I take it Tom Morrow's parents didn't like him much?"

"Why would you say that?"

Set Up

"Tom Morrow? His name is like a hyphenated 'tomorrow.'"

Roland's brows lifted. "You're right. That's funny. Never thought of it that way."

I gripped the hand that was between my thighs a moment ago. "Don't tell me you had this hand up a horse's ass."

He shook his head. "No, it was the other hand."

"Eww, and you've been touching me." I knew he wore gloves, and Roland was like Mr. Clean when it came to infection control, but I liked to razz him.

"I've got another glove in the truck if you're interested."

"I don't think I need my tonsils tickled rectally." I sipped the wine and licked the moisture from my lips.

His eyes trailed the movement of my tongue, and his blue eyes sparkled. "How hungry are you?"

"I'm starving." At the same time his shoulders slumped, I pulled a twenty from my purse and tossed it on the table. "I'll race you to your place. You can feed me there." I was out of the booth in seconds, and he was hot on my heels.

Chapter 25

NATALIE

Waking up to Roland was amazing; being sandwiched between him and Pepper, not so much. I pressed my hands against the furry coat and pushed him off the bed. He slunk to the floor and crawled on top of the dog bed Roland had put in the corner like it was some sort of punishment.

"Good morning," Roland said in a slow, sexy voice. The kind of gravelly tone that made me forget we made love three times last night. The low humming sound that made me want him again despite my tired, aching body.

I stretched my arms above my head and reached for nirvana, that feeling you get when the stretch makes your body sing. "Good morning." The sheet fell to my waist, exposing my breasts to the cold morning air.

Roland didn't miss the pucker of my nipples. He rolled over and drew lazy circles around them without actually touching the needy nubs.

"Are you hungry?" His question was loaded.

"Ravenous." No matter how close he was to me, I wanted more. I needed more. I hungered for his touch.

"You've got to be sore."

"Yep." I rolled his direction and ran my hand over his chest. He was an amusement park for my fingers. All the hills and valleys and curves created an addictive joy ride. "It doesn't stop me from wanting you."

"You're insatiable." He rolled me over and straddled my body. His now hardened length pressed between my thighs.

"I can't help myself, I'm a Roland addict."

God, the man was stunning. His Caribbean blue eyes turned to deep sapphire when he was aroused, and this morning they were almost black. On any other man, I would have been frightened by the intensity, but with Roland, those dark, passionate orbs only increased my desire.

"I'm happy to be your fix." He pulled a condom from the nightstand and ripped open the foil.

The latex had barely hit his skin when the sound of an ambulance shrilled from his phone. Roland was organized, even down to his ringtones. That sound meant a pet emergency.

He hopped from between my legs and picked up his phone. "Dr. Mallory."

By the way his shoulders slumped forward, I knew our morning play was finished and Roland would be called to a different type of action.

I rolled from the bed and pulled on the shirt he wore the night before. It came down to my knees, but it smelled of him, and I loved being wrapped in his scent. Yes, I had fallen in love with Roland Mallory, but was he in love with me? Ever since that night he told me he could love me, he had never announced that he did.

I was at the coffee pot when Roland hung up the phone.

"Problem?"

"A client's about forty minutes out."

"Okay." I pressed the start button, and the machine hissed and whined, then spit black gold into a mug.

"Are you okay?"

He rubbed his hand down my back. He was way too perceptive when it came to my moods. I had all these emotions boiling inside me. I was aroused, I was in love, and I was confused, and Roland probably picked up on all of them.

I turned around and looked at him. It was hard to ask a serious question with him standing in front of me naked, but I needed to know. "Why do you like me?"

His eyes roamed my body. The silence between us was unbearable. What if it was only sex? "Tell me something good." One moment passed, followed by another, and another, until I was ready to burst out of my skin if he didn't say something soon.

I heaved a sigh of exasperation. "Come on, there has to be something you like about me. You spend enough time with me." I chewed at my thumbnail. If I could have afforded a manicure, this nail would have been white-tipped and impervious to my gnawing.

He took his time to respond. A slow, sexy smile spread across his full lips. "I like your kisses."

"Just my kisses?" I asked indignantly.

He leaned in and pulled me closer. "I like the way you smell of oranges."

"That's just my shampoo. Anyone could smell like oranges." My lips drooped into a pout.

Roland gripped my hips. "I like your body. I like the sounds you make when I'm inside you. I like being inside you." By now his entire body leaned into me, and his head was pressed against my chest. "I like these." He rubbed his face back and forth over the swell of my breasts.

"You're a man. I don't know many who don't like the feel of a woman's breasts or the sensation of sinking inside her body." Lord, was that all he liked? Disappointment churned in my stomach.

"I'm not like all men." Quick and seamless, he lifted me into his arms, and I wrapped my legs around his waist. "Most men would have taken you up on the offer of your body that first night. I waited."

"How chivalrous of you." Sarcasm oozed from me. "You waited three days."

He bit his lip and narrowed his eyes—his damn fuck-me eyes. Just looking at them made me want to drag him back to bed. It was that or rush to Tiffany's for a treat. Didn't I deserve a treat? I had cooked and cleaned all week.

"I read three dates is the magic number." He buried his face in my neck and nipped at the skin just under my ear. Desire pounded through my veins louder than the bass at a techno concert. My body hummed and throbbed, driven by the relentless assault he waged on my emotions.

His lips brushed against my skin, sending whimpers of desire straight to my core, but he wasn't answering my question. If sex was all there was to us, I needed to know—each day he took my body, he also captured a piece of my heart.

I slid down his body and separated his fire from my skin. "Where did you read that?"

"In *Cosmo*." He said it like everyone read the magazine.

"You read *Cosmo*?" *What man buys Cosmo?*

He gripped my hips and tugged me close. Any closer, and we'd be using the same set of lungs.

"I buy it for the office. My female clients like it. Speaking of female clients, Terra Rodgers is on her way over with Princess."

"I don't like Terra Rodgers." Last time I'd seen her at the office, she'd claimed she was there for shots, but I was sure she came for Roland.

"How can you not like Terra? She's the sweetest."

I snorted and pushed back on his chest. "She's a viper wrapped in cotton candy. Not even the good pink kind, but the blue kind that stains your fingers and teeth."

Roland's body shuddered with laughter.

"Don't you laugh! That woman rubbed her fun bags all over your arm on the pretense of reaching for a pen."

Roland pinched my chin and held it there. "Fun bags? The only fun bags I'm interested in playing with are yours. Are you jealous?"

Frustrated with the conversation, I whipped my chin from his grip. I was fishing for something to make me feel less insecure about our relationship, and all I got was the fact that he liked to fuck. I was paraphrasing for sure, but since our argument last week, Roland hadn't mentioned the word 'love' once. Why was that?

"Yes, Roland, I'm jealous. I don't like other women touching what belongs to me."

"I belong to you?" He gave me a smirk I wanted to slap straight off his face.

"Grrrrrr, yes, you belong to me." I played with the buttons on the shirt I wore. His hands slid around my waist and slipped down to grip my bottom.

"Is it just sex for you?" There it was, finally out in the open. It took ten minutes of conversation to get to this place—to my need-to-know place.

His tongue flicked out to wet his lips. "I like the sex." He gripped my hips and held me in place. "I like that you're here in my house. I like that you unpacked; it says that you plan to stay long enough to get to know me. I like that you're trying hard to please me. Did I say I like the sex?"

Exasperated, I shook my head so hard, I thought my eyeballs would roll out. "Yes, you said you like the sex."

All humor left his face, and sincerity took its place. "I like all that, but it's not why I'm here with you."

"No?" I pulled my thumbnail to my mouth and nibbled.

"No. I met this girl who fell out of a truck. She might as well have fallen from heaven. She's as beautiful as an angel, but she's also the devil."

I'd been called a lot of things in my life, but never Satan. I tried to slide away from him, but he held me tight.

"Stay and hear me out." He lifted his hand and brushed back my bangs. "She has this idea that money would make her happy. I wasn't sure about her motives at first. She wanted what she wanted, and I didn't know if I was in her sights because I was a vet or because I had a dick. She was a pain in the ass, but we had this chemistry. Then again, so did Chernobyl."

"You're comparing us to a nuclear disaster?"

"Yes, but it's a beautiful disaster." He moved his hands to my shoulders and massaged the wire-tight stress away. "You can learn a lot from a catastrophe."

I tilted my head like a confused puppy. I wasn't sure I liked where this conversation was going. So far I'd been called an angel, a devil, and now a catastrophe. "Finish so I can decide if I want to kill you or kiss you."

"Don't rush me, we're having a moment."

"It's a moment all right, but it might be your last." I looked at the clock on his wall. "Besides, you have an emergency on the way."

"You're my most pressing emergency." He chuckled and traced his finger down the plunging neckline of my shirt. "You aren't anything like I thought you were. You're so much better. My negative opinion of you changed with that dog." He pointed to the corner.

Pepper lifted his head. I swear, his comprehension skills rivaled those of a five-year-old.

"Your opinion of me changed because of Pepper?" If only my mother could be so easily influenced.

"Not at first. I couldn't figure out what your angle was. I saw you outside with him, and you were trying to do right by him. I knew then he wasn't a short-term pet. He'd eaten your shoes, but you kept him."

"I threatened to take him back."

"Yes, but you weren't serious."

Little did he know, I had been as serious as Ebola, but my shoes were a small sacrifice to pay for the bigger picture—my inheritance. And now that Pepper had been around for a while, I couldn't imagine my life without him.

"Okay, so you like my dog and sex."

"Be careful how you word that; people go to jail for that kind of stuff."

"Are you going to get to the point?"

"Yes, I am." He lifted my chin so I was forced to look up to him. I loved his height. When I stood, my head cradled perfectly between the muscles of his chest. "You've shown me who you are and who you're not. You're not a girl driven by money, like I thought. You're a woman driven by the desire to find herself. I don't like you, Natalie."

My breath held. Was that it? He didn't like me?

"Natalie, I'm falling in love with you."

A whoosh of air released, and my heart raced to catch the beats it missed. I wanted Roland to believe I was the girl he was falling in love with. I wanted to be her. Had I become her?

"Thanks for giving me a chance, Roland."

"Everyone gets one with me." He'd said that before. One chance was all a person got. If they blew it, what then?

I pushed my body into his. The touch of his skin was almost as powerful as his words. He was falling in love with me.

As hard as it was for me to send him away, I did. "You should take a shower." The last thing I wanted was for my man to be naked when Terra Rodgers showed up.

His hand rubbed down the soft cotton of his shirt and rested on my bottom. "Can I have a rain check for this morning?"

"As long as you love me, you can have anything you want."

"Be careful, Natalie, I can want a lot." The damn man winked and walked his naked ass into the bathroom, leaving me wanting a lot of what he offered.

Fifteen minutes later, the front door buzzed. I'd dressed in yesterday's clothes. Since Roland was finishing up in the bathroom, Pepper and I decided to greet our nemesis.

Her expression couldn't hide the shock when she saw me. I'd known the woman was attracted to Roland, and now I knew I'd thwarted her plans.

"Oh, wow, I didn't expect him to call in the help."

She had that same haughty demeanor as Victoria Kincaid. Each time I was exposed to it, I died a little inside. How had I lived in that poisonous shell for so long? Instead of engaging her, though, I smiled.

"Dr. Mallory will be out in a second. What's up with Princess?"

She rolled her eyes at me. "Like I told Roland—" she purred his name, and my claws itched to scratch her eyes out "—she had blood on her mouth."

"Okay, let me get an exam room ready. I'll be right back." I glanced to my side, and Pepper was lying down next to my chair.

Set Up

How in the hell had I gotten so lucky with him? "Be good," I told him before I walked away.

Moments later, a scream came from the lobby. Terra Rodgers was hysterical. "Stop it! Stop it!"

I grabbed for the nearest weapon I could find. Robyn had trained me to look for two things when I entered a room. The first was an exit, and the second was a weapon. Terra's scream sounded like someone was assaulting her, so I picked up the plastic heartworm model, thinking I could use it as a club, I ran into the lobby.

In the center of the room was Pepper mounting Princess. While Terra screamed about rape, Roland—who'd come running at the sound of the shrieks—waited with me for the mating to end. There was nothing to be done but damage control.

Chapter 26

NATALIE

It took an hour to negotiate paternity responsibility. Terra claimed innocence for Princess, and Pepper was found guilty of sexual assault. In the end, we negotiated a truce based on the following conditions.

Pepper would be neutered that afternoon.

Roland would provide veterinarian care for Princess.

Any puppies to come from the unfortunate union would be my responsibility.

Most importantly, Roland's reputation would remain intact.

I LOOKED over at Pepper lying in his bed. His head hung low over the cushion. "He looks miserable." The poor dog hadn't looked that sad when I rescued him.

"I'd be miserable, too, if I just got laid and you cut my nuts off."

"I'm sorry, Roland, I should have been watching him." I should have known as soon as I said, 'Be good', things would go to hell in a handbasket. The last time I'd told the damn dog to behave, he'd eaten all my shoes.

"You can't blame him. She is a sexy yellow Lab." We moved around the kitchen together. He was gathering napkins and drinks while I plated the pizza we ordered.

"Yes, it's a shame her mother has the face of a pug and the brain of a peanut." I walked to the sofa and plopped myself down.

"They say the breed is so ugly, it's cute." He took a seat beside me.

"You can't possibly think she's cute. Especially after that tirade." My stomach grumbled. I was famished. One cup of coffee didn't hold a girl for long.

"I never did think she was cute. I'm attracted to your type."

"What type is that?"

"Oh, you know, irresponsible felons who worm their way into my heart."

"Tell me what you told me this morning." I was fishing again. When had I become this needy girl? Probably when I found out I was never who I thought I was.

"That I like sex?" He waggled his brows at me and gave me the male equivalent of a come-hither look.

"No, the part that came after that."

"Oh, the part where I told you I liked that you adopted a dog?" He took a bite of his pizza and ignored my growl. "Or was it the part where I said I liked the smell of your shampoo?"

"You're an asshole."

He tossed his plate to the table and straddled my lap. I was so stunned by his quickness, I choked on my last bite of pizza. "Do you remember what happened the last time you called me an asshole?"

I did remember. He claimed the title proudly, then he claimed my mouth, and if it hadn't been for the jingling of Rick's keys over our heads, he might have claimed my body against the wall of the bar.

"Mmm hmmm," I hummed into his mouth.

He carried me to his bed, and that's where we stayed for the next day. God, I loved that man, and he loved my body so good.

I ARRIVED BACK at my cabin on Monday night. Mickey was standing by the barn wearing jeans, a plaid shirt, and a frown. The planning of the junior rodeo had taken its toll on her. Thank goodness it would be over this weekend and she could get back to her normal life.

"Natalie!" she yelled from across the field. "Wait up." That wasn't the sound of a girl who wanted coffee and chitchat. She marched toward me with purpose. Her hair whipped around her face like an angry cyclone.

"I'm so mad at you." Her fury shook me. I had no clue what had prompted the outburst.

"Why?"

She pulled a folded paper from her back pocket and waved it around. "Did you make the deposit?"

My stomach coiled, and bile rose to my throat. "Oh. My. God. I forgot." I left Pepper in the car and ran for my cabin. Inside, still sitting on the counter, were the prepared deposit bags. Two of them, one for payroll and one for the business checking.

She followed me inside and slapped the folded piece of paper on the counter. "As of now, you owe me $175 in overdraft fees. How could you let that happen?"

"I was preoccupied. I'm sorry." I ran to my room and pulled two hundred dollar bills from the envelope that held my dwindling resources. "I'll take it now." I pressed the bills into her palm.

"Yes, you will, and tomorrow, instead of burying your head in my screwed up finances, you'll be hand-delivering apologies to the distributors I use. You'll be begging them to deliver the goods I need for the rodeo."

"Oh shit."

"'Oh shit' is right. Will you ever consider anyone's needs before your own?" She turned on the heels of her boots and headed for the door.

"You're not being fair. It was an honest mistake." I gathered the bags from the counter. "Why didn't you call me?"

"You don't have a phone!" she screamed.

"I was with Roland. You could have called his office."

Mickey shook her head. "That's where you and I are different. I would never interrupt his business to save mine."

With my arms wrapped tightly around the deposit bags, I skirted past her. "I'm taking care of it."

"Natalie, you better hope you can fix this, because if my reputation goes south due to your selfishness, I'll never forgive you."

Roland's statement about getting one chance echoed in my mind. I had to fix this. I refused to let Mickey or anyone else down.

It took a lifetime at the bank to get the after-hours drop box to swallow the bags. The first one got stuck, and it took ten minutes of shaking to set it free. The bank really needed to fix this problem. A girl could get mugged trying to make things right.

My heart thumped against its cage when I drove onto the ranch. Would Mickey be waiting with her arms crossing her chest and a scowl crossing her face?

Roland's truck was parked in front of the stables, and next to it he stood with Mickey. Both of their expressions were grim. *Shit.* I was transported back in time to second grade, when I'd written on the bathroom stall that Katrina Cage stuffed her bra. What had I been thinking? No second grader wore a bra. When I was called to the office, Principal Anderson and my father greeted me, and they held the same grim expressions now pasted on Roland and Mickey's faces.

"Let's go, Pepper." My poor puppy was still walking gingerly. "Love hurts, right boy?" I looked over my shoulder toward Roland. His look of displeasure made my stomach churn.

In minutes, Roland was by my side. He was a combination of understanding and soft rebuke. "You can't blame her."

"I blame you. If you didn't addle my mind so much, I might have had two cells to rub together to remind me what I needed to do." I poured us both a glass of wine. I needed to settle my nerves. For a moment, I'd thought Mickey was going to kick me out.

"I'm not taking the blame for this. I've already taken on the responsibility of one of your oversights." His eyes went straight to Pepper.

"Really? You're going to blame him knocking up the Labrador on me?"

Roland stared at me with a grim reaper look. "I was in the shower. You were supposed to watch him."

I huffed out a breath and walked to the fireplace to grab Bo Bo. He never blamed me for anything. "All right. I've screwed up."

"You need to get a phone."

I wanted to scream. Now that I'd paid Mickey back for the overdrafts, I only had a few hundred dollars left. I glanced down at my toes. Maybe I shouldn't have splurged on a pedicure.

"I can't afford a phone."

"I'll buy you one."

"You can't afford to buy me a phone. I've seen your finances." Was this what being working class felt like? Was it a struggle to survive every day? Once again, I hung my head in shame. I'd never considered anyone's needs above my wants.

"I can afford a phone more than I can afford career suicide. If this rodeo fails, both my reputation and Mickey's are shot."

"That seems like an exaggeration. It's a bunch of kids from 4-H."

"Grow up, Natalie. It's more than that, and you know it. It will be a public flaying if we can't deliver what we promised."

"I'll take care of it."

I had no idea how I would fix it, but tomorrow morning I'd dress in my best Western wear and sweet talk anyone who would listen to me. A smile and an apology were all I had to offer. I hoped it would be enough.

IT WAS five o'clock when I dragged my tired body from the car and walked into my cabin. The day had been a success, but not without sacrifice. It would appear that bouncing a check was frowned upon, and not even my brightest smile could allay the fears that Mickey was running a shoddy production, but everyone came on board with their support.

Set Up

The ranch supply store was the hardest sell, and it wasn't until I agreed to man the kissing booth for an hour that the owner relented and decided to reinstate his support for the fundraiser. No doubt the old coot would be first in line with a handful of dollar bills.

Pepper and I lumbered into the kitchen, where his kibble was stored. As he gobbled down his dinner, I slapped some peanut butter and jelly on toast. Pepper followed me like a shadow to the couch.

Roland wouldn't be over tonight. He had driven to Durango to pick up a rescue. Why did people purchase pets they didn't intend to keep?

I looked down at Pepper lying over my feet and realized I was a hypocrite. I'd used this animal for my own purposes, fully intending to dispose of him when I got what I was after. Here he sat curled up next to me like I was the best thing since that little yellow Lab he had fun with. No matter what I did to Pepper, whether it was forget to feed him or yell at him for wanting to go outside, he never judged me and never gave up on me. He gave his love unconditionally.

I stood up and walked to the fireplace, where Bo Bo sat in a place of honor. I picked up the sock monkey and pulled him into my arms. He was there on my darkest days. He held all my secrets. He was the sounding board for all my hurts, and his scratchy material had dried up a lake of tears over the years, but today I would share my joy.

I patted the sofa next to me. Pepper eyed me with caution. "It's all right. You sneak into our bed. Surely, you can snuggle with me now." He gave me an if-I-must look and climbed on the cushion beside me, where he sat patiently while I told Bo Bo about him and Roland and the girls at the ranch until I tired and fell asleep.

Sometime in the middle of the night, strong hands lifted me. I didn't panic. I knew the feel of those hands. Roland's scent wrapped around me as he carried me to bed.

"What are you doing here?" Sleep slurred my voice.

"I couldn't stand to spend the night without you." He stripped me out of my clothes and stared long and hard at me.

"I'm glad you're here."

I turned over to watch him undress. Looking at Roland was a

guilty pleasure—my own private strip show. He crossed his arms at the hem of his shirt and pulled it over his head. Every ripple from his shoulders to his hips flexed and tightened under my gaze.

"Stop looking at me like that." He popped the button of his jeans and yanked the zipper down.

"Like what?" My sleepy voice purred. A moonbeam slivered through a crack in the curtains and highlighted his body. In the shadows of the night, Roland crawled into bed beside me.

"Like you want to eat me alive." His hands roamed over me, igniting every burning nerve ending.

A giggle burst forth. "I'm not into raw meat," I teased.

He nudged my knees apart and climbed between my legs. "I'll make you change your mind."

"I'll enjoy you trying." I wrapped my legs around him and pulled him deep inside me.

"Damn," he hissed. "I need a condom, baby. Otherwise, you're going to be just like Terra's Labrador retriever." He tried to pull out.

I gripped him tighter, not willing to let him go just yet. "Give me a minute to feel completely part of you." Condoms were fine, but there was nothing as amazing as feeling every vein and ripple of Roland slide in and out of me.

He growled, but he gave me what I wanted. The friction of his thick cock forced an orgasm to rock through my body. I cried out as the spasms vibrated through me, then noodled beneath him.

"Damn it, Natalie, you're making me lose my mind." He pumped into me several more times before he pulled out and spilled his heat over my stomach. His body fell to my side. "That was very unwise for both of us."

I knew he was right, but it felt good to be close to him, to share something I never shared with another. "I wanted you to be my first."

He chuckled. "Well, we both know that wasn't going to happen. You've been consorting with Ryan Gosling for years." He pulled a few tissues from the box next to the bed and cleaned up my stomach.

"I meant—"

Set Up

"I know what you meant." He wrapped a leg around mine and pulled me close to him. "I'm honored. And Natalie—" he sucked in a breath "—I could love you, too."

I fell asleep in the arms of the man I knew I was already hopelessly in love with. I only hoped I could convince him to love me back.

Chapter 27

NATALIE

The coffee was steaming and the eggs were almost done when Roland walked into the kitchen all wet and sexy. He smelled like a citrus grove.

"How come you're up so early?"

I plopped microwaved bacon on the plates and put them on the table. "I couldn't sleep, so I thought I'd try to make you breakfast." I looked at the plates with pride. The eggs were cooked through without any brown or black bits.

"Natalie, you amaze me. Look at how far you've come from almost killing me with that first casserole." He sat at his seat and picked up his fork.

I watched in anticipation. It was only eggs, but it was the first meal I didn't burn or undercook. After the first chicken fail, I tried again the next day. Who knew you could burn and undercook a chicken at the same time? I thought it would cook faster at five hundred degrees. The outside looked crisp and amazing, but the inside was like a murder scene the minute we cut into it.

"I'm trying."

He swallowed his first bite and sipped at his coffee. "It's perfect, Natalie."

Set Up

I had done a lot of things in my life. I'd traveled the world. I'd slept with every man I set my sights on. I'd won pageants and graduated college with honors. But watching Roland enjoy a breakfast I made for him was by far a crowning achievement.

Sitting here eating breakfast was such a couple thing to do. In the past few weeks, Roland's life and mine had become entwined. Between him and everyone at the ranch, I got to see firsthand what a family should look like. Roland made me want to be a better person.

We talked about the next few days while we ate. The Junior Rodeo had everyone on pins and needles. The community was abuzz about the generosity of Dr. Roland Mallory and Mickey at M and M Ranch. So much could go wrong, and so much could go right. And the reputations of both Mickey and Roland were on the line.

Like a family, we gathered our things and left for work. Pepper lagged behind, carrying Bo Bo gently in his mouth. He must have found him on the couch. My first instinct was to grab the stuffed pet and put him back on the mantel, but the way Pepper carried him showed a level of respect. This wasn't a shoe he was destroying, but rather a treasure he was protecting.

THE NEXT THREE days flew by in a blur. The ranch was a bustle of activity. Vendors set up food stands. Ranchers brought livestock that were housed in temporary pens around the property.

If I thought Toby was annoying with his hammer, nothing was worse than that damn rooster that showed up two days ago. Needless to say, Roland had been well-sexed and fed since its arrival. What was left to do but cook and make love when I was up and couldn't get back to sleep?

"What can I do to help?"

I tied a bandana around Pepper's neck. Today was the big day, and I wanted him dressed for the occasion. We had matching red bandanas. His was strictly for fashion. Mine was doused in sanitizer so I could wipe my lips between kissers.

"You want to help me? Then don't man the kissing booth."

"I have to. The old goat from the supply store made it part of the agreement. He delivered all the supplies like he said he would, and now I have to hold up my end of the bargain. You can't tell me how important reputation is to you and expect me to ignore mine."

"It's your reputation I'm concerned about." He smiled sweetly, but there was a hint of mischievousness glinting through his expression. "How am I supposed to feel about all these men kissing what's mine?"

"Yours?" I cocked my head and grabbed the leash from the door. Pepper didn't really need it, but with so many people milling around the ranch today, I thought it safer to keep him tethered to me.

"Are you having some doubt as to who you belong to? I could take you back into the bedroom and show you one more time."

I loved it when he went caveman and got possessive of me. Never in my life had I felt as valued as I did around Roland. He had a way of making me feel like I mattered. "You don't have time. Your free clinic starts in ten minutes."

He turned his eyes toward me. "Be here at noon so I can remind you." He grumbled in frustration and adjusted his pants. "And…if I see Cole within a hundred yards of you, I'm going to kick his ass."

"Oh my God, really?" I heaved out an exasperated breath. "I told you he helped pull my car from the ditch the night you were such an animalistic asshole at the bar."

"Yes, and I appreciate that, but he doesn't need to touch you. Only I get to do that."

"You know you're being ridiculous, right?"

"Yes, I do, and I find great satisfaction in getting you flustered. It brings the color out in your cheeks and puts a fire in you that shows up later in bed." He pressed his lips to mine in a dramatic, passion-filled kiss—the kind of kiss that skirted down my spine and curled my toes.

"Don't forget, Natalie, I could love you." He rushed out the

Set Up

door and disappeared into the crowd of people already gathering around the ranch.

I'll make you love me.

It was funny how we never acknowledged that the love was already there. It was as if he didn't want me to stop trying, so he never said the words "I love you." His terms of endearment were always something just out of reach but within sight. Maybe it was too soon. Three weeks wasn't much time, but we'd spent every minute possible together, and that brought us close. Besides, we hadn't killed each other, so that was something.

Because I would be taking care of finances here later, Pepper and I locked up the cabin as we left. I didn't want another problem that connected money and my name. I did have a reputation—I was a thief—and it would take me a long time and a lot of good deeds to overcome that.

We walked around the ranch and took in all the happenings. In the stables behind the cabins, real cowboys were giving roping classes. Toby and Cole were among the stars.

In a small enclosure out front, Megan was giving pony rides on a tiny horse they called Princess. What those little people riding didn't know was Princess was actually a boy. I hoped the kids didn't get a close look between the horse's legs. It was important for kids to make-believe, and if they wanted to pretend he was a princess, then so be it. Lord knows I'd gotten hit with reality way too young. When I should have been riding ponies, I was burying an empty casket and saying farewell to a normal childhood.

In the barn, Roland's free clinic was ten kids deep. Everything from kittens to lizards was present. When I walked in, his eyes met mine. They held a promise of passion later. I looked at my watch and sighed. It would be hours before he could make good on that promise. I blew him a kiss and walked toward the birthing stalls, where Keagan was explaining to old and young alike about the process of breeding horses.

I left them and walked to the stables. It smelled like fresh hay and leather—smells that were offensive initially and now felt like home. Holly sat on a chair in the corner, making sure no one teased the boarders.

"You doing okay?" I asked.

"Yes, isn't this an amazing day?"

"It is. Who knew I lived in the presence of such greatness?" I leaned against the wall where Roland and I had almost had sex for the first time. There was something about him and walls, apparently—first it was the bar, then the stables.

"I don't see you much. How are you doing?" She stood up and stretched. If you didn't know she was pregnant, you would have mistaken her little mound for a few extra pounds.

"I'm really good. I work for Roland, and all things Roland are amazing." Talk about opposites attracting. He was everything good, and I was everything else.

"There's some kind of love bug on this ranch. It takes a bite of you, and you're gone for good."

We weren't moving around, so Pepper took a seat next to me. "It's hit me hard. First with this dog," I leaned over and pet his soft ears, "then with Roland. He's a man I could fall in love with."

"'Could'?" Her expression was soft. "You turn to putty at the mention of his name."

"It's still early, don't you think?"

"You're talking to the wrong girl. I was out of prison, back in prison, out again, married, and knocked up before the seasons could change."

"Okay, then, if we're confessing, I'm hopelessly in love with him. Who would have thought I'd trade sports cars and fine dining for a man who spends his days talking to animals?"

"Well, those are just his days. I'm pretty sure he spends his nights differently."

I could feel the heat rise to my cheeks. After spending over a thousand days in prison, I had a deficit to make up for when it came to sex. Poor Roland didn't get much sleep these days. "I won't kiss and tell, but I can sum it up in one word: amazing."

"Speak of the devil himself." Holly looked toward the entrance, where my Nordic god was entering. He walked with purpose straight to me.

"What are you doing here? I thought you were shoving thermometers up unsuspecting kittens' bottoms?"

"I'm finished for now and figured I'd find my kitten." At this point, he was standing in front of us, pulling me into his arms. "Hate to interrupt you, Holly, but my girl here has some unfinished business." He lifted me into his arms and started walking toward the exit. Pepper followed obediently, dragging his leash behind him.

"Oh my God, you basically told her we were going to go back to the cabin to do the dirty."

"Sweetheart, Holly can't say much. In her state, she's hardly a virgin."

Holly laughed so hard and long, I heard her halfway back to the cabin.

"You're awful. You're giving me a reputation."

"Are we back to the reputation conversation?" He held me while I unlocked the cabin door.

"Yes. What are people going to say about me after you basically carried me here? Did you hear all those hoots and hollers? They know what we're doing in here." I slid down his body until my feet hit the floor.

"They know you belong to me. That will keep half of them from the kissing booth."

"Oh my God, you are so selfish." I wiggled against him and began to unbutton his lab jacket. Undressing Roland was like unwrapping a package on Christmas Day. I knew there was something good inside. "How much time do you have?"

"I'm all yours, baby. What did you have in mind?" He was a master at undressing me. Nimble fingers had my pants off in seconds. It was obvious what he had in mind by the part of my body he exposed first.

"You and me against this wall." I tapped my knuckles against the logs that scratched at my back.

"Gladly." He kicked his pants to the side and rolled a condom onto his more than ready erection. "You spoiled me the other night. When do you think you can get on birth control so we can do without these?" He lined up and pressed against me. He had a way of teasing me that nearly took me to the edge before he gave me even an inch of himself.

"If my boss can do without me for an hour or so Monday morning, I have an appointment for that very thing."

He lifted my hips and pressed into me. *I'll never get over the feeling of him filling me up like he does*, I thought hazily. Each time we connected, my heart swelled. It was a love squeeze that linked me to this man in ways more than our bodies. He'd given me so much. He'd given me his time, his attention, and his passion. Although we were lying to each other about our feelings, I felt his love.

"Natalie, you're amazing." He stroked me gently until I whimpered his name. When he shuddered inside me, I held on to him tightly. These moments connected me to something real. I'd give up everything to have an endless supply of Roland.

It was no accident he found me before lunch. After we fed our sexual appetites, Roland made sandwiches and fed my stomach. We curled up on the couch and snuggled until it was time for me to man the kissing booth.

"I smell like sex."

"You smell like me, and that will keep all the horny men away from you."

"Are you jealous?"

He pulled his lower lip between his teeth and nodded his head. "I'd be an idiot to not mark you before you went out there."

I exaggerated a growl. "Such a caveman."

He stood up and pounded his chest. "Got your sanitizer?"

He led me and Pepper to the kissing booth, where this year's rodeo queen was waiting for me to relieve her. I doused my bandana until it hung in a limp, wet mess, but I was ready.

Roland stood off to the side like a sentry while I gave impersonal kisses to several dozen men for a buck apiece. When Cole approached, Roland pointed to him and told him to move along.

The rest of the day, we visited the events. Mickey gave a demonstration on barrel racing. Kerrick offered a weapons safety class.

Set Up

Killian showed his skills at taming a horse. Holly had moved to the arena, where one of her last-wish clients got personalized treatment from Keagan. Keagan had set up the young man dying of cancer in a special saddle that supported him so he could ride out onto the range and live a dream.

SUNDAY WAS A REPEAT OF SATURDAY, except for the absence of the kissing booth. For the most part, I spent the day inside doing the books for the event—my contribution.

I thought about my mother and how proud I hoped she would be of me. Not because I wanted my inheritance, but because I was a part of something bigger than myself. I had become a valuable member of a family—the ranch family.

Chapter 28

NATALIE

I shoved and tugged at the night deposit box until I heard the clunk of the bag hit the bottom. I would have taken it inside, but the bank didn't open until nine, and I had that oh-so-important appointment. I'd researched all options, and the IUD was the one that would allow me to get the desired experience with Roland immediately.

"That's a lovely watch," the doctor said as she did her business between my legs. We could have been sitting at a coffee shop with the way this conversation was going.

"Thanks. It's a family heirloom."

She warned me of an upcoming pinch. "I'd never take that sucker off my wrist."

"I never plan to. It took too much to get it to let it out of my sight." I rubbed the diamonds that circled the face and smiled. The journey had come at a great price, but in the end it was worth it. If I ended up with nothing other than Roland and my ranch family, I was far richer than most.

"Okay, we're done here."

"That's it?"

"Easy peasy."

Set Up

I paid the small co-pay required by the 'free clinic' and raced to the office. Hopefully, Roland's schedule wasn't too busy and we could test out my new equipment right away.

When I arrived, Pepper danced with excitement around my legs. The lobby was full of people and their pets. After the weekend, word had spread about Roland's vet skills, and the walk-ins were abundant. A look of relief washed over Roland's face the minute he saw me.

"I'm so glad you're here."

He rushed to me and pressed a kiss to my lips. It was the first workplace affection he'd ever shown. We might have spent our lunch hours making love in his little studio in the back, but once we stepped outside the door, it was all business, with the exception of a longing look or soft touch here and there.

By closing time, we had seen two rabbits, a parakeet, five dogs, a kitten, and a bearded dragon. We didn't bother going back to the ranch. We turned off the phones and went straight to bed. In the afterglow, we held each other and talked.

"I love that nothing is coming between us."

Roland brushed my damp hair from my face and looked at me with so much love, I almost couldn't breathe—but even though we no longer used a condom, there were things coming between us.

Confident that we were in a good place in our relationship, I began to confess. "Don't hate me, but I wasn't completely honest when I first met you."

His body stiffened. "What do you mean?" He leaned back and narrowed his eyes at me.

I pressed closer to him and rubbed my palms across his chest. Under my touch, he relaxed. "Nothing big, just that everything I did initially was all about gaining my mother's trust. Everything but you, that is. You were an unexpected bonus."

He separated his body from mine and once again stared me down. "This sounds like a serious conversation. Should we get dressed?"

"No." I pulled him closer to me and yanked the cover over our shoulders. "I just wanted to clear the air." A lump took up residence in my throat. "You mentioned that nothing is coming between us, but there's one thing that keeps niggling at me."

"Is this a confession?"

"Yes." I brought my thumbnail to my mouth and started gnawing at the corner.

"Spill it."

I inhaled deeply and exhaled slowly. "I didn't initially get Pepper because I wanted to make a difference in his life. I got him so he could make a difference in mine."

Roland chuckled. "That's usually the way it works out."

At the mention of his name, Pepper climbed onto the bed and shimmied between us.

"No, you don't understand. My mother is holding my inheritance hostage until I can make a difference in something or someone's life. I was using Pepper to prove something to her."

"Natalie, I think you proved something to yourself instead. Do you love the dog?"

I looked down at the puppy that changed my life. "I love him more than money, and less than I could love you."

"Good to hear." He leaned in and nipped at my lip. "Is that all?"

"No, I took this job because it was also part of my plan. So was working on the fundraiser."

He cupped my cheek and smiled. "And now?"

"I love working here, and I hope you'll keep me on board."

"Do you love working here more than you could love me?" He tilted his head and gave me a tell-me-the-truth look.

"Never."

"Good, because I don't know how to compete with a job. Is there anything else?"

"No. Isn't that enough?"

"There's nothing that can come between us."

He twined his fingers through my hair and tugged it tight to hold me in place. The way he touched me made my eyes close, my breath quicken, and my heart beat in double time. I swear to God, my body heated until I was molten liquid and became a part of him.

Set Up

DESPITE HOW CLOSE I was feeling to Roland and how much I didn't want to leave him, I had to go to the ranch to work on the books. Tuesdays belonged to Mickey. This was a big week for everyone. Friday, I was meeting Mom about my inheritance and would miss my afternoon ranch shift.

As I pulled up, everything looked to be back to normal. The vendors were gone, as were the temporary livestock pens. I was crossing my fingers that the damn rooster was sold as well.

The whole affair was a major success. Mickey and Roland had raised over $28,000 for the two charities. The press would be here tomorrow morning to record the presentation of the donation.

When I pulled in front of my cabin, my heart lurched forward. Mickey was sitting in the porch swing with a grimace pasted to her face. I hopped out and called for Pepper to follow me.

"Where is it?" Mickey yelled.

"What are you talking about?" I tapped my thigh, and Pepper moved in close. Something told me I was going to need his support.

"The deposit, Natalie." Mickey stopped the swing and stood up. Her anger made her look tall and imposing, when in reality she was at least an inch shorter than me. "I checked my bank balance, and the deposit hasn't been made. I have to write two checks tomorrow I can't afford to cash if that money doesn't make it into my account. How could you do this again?" Her face looked like an unhappy, wilted beet—all red and crinkled.

All the air was sucked from around me, and the world began to tilt. I reached down to touch Pepper and steady myself. "I made the deposit yesterday. I swear."

"Forgive me if I don't believe you. The numbers in my account are currently the only truth I can rely on. Where's the money, Natalie? It's not in my account, so it has to be somewhere."

I stumbled forward at her words. They were laced with more disappointment than anger, but they were also filled with fear. "I'll take care of it."

Mickey stepped down the stairs, then turned back to me. "You have less than twenty-four hours to come up with the deposit. Failure to do so will ruin both my reputation and Roland's. Figure it out, Natalie; you've already had your one pass—I'm not giving you another. Anything less than a complete fix is unacceptable." She kicked up the dust as she stalked toward her home.

How did my life get so screwed up? This morning I was making love to the only man I've ever loved, and now I had to figure out how not to lose the best life I've ever had.

My first stop was the bank. After an interminable wait, I was ushered into a room where I completely broke down into a blubbering mess while I explained the situation to a woman who appeared unaffected by my distress.

Fifteen tissues and a bottle of water later, I left, dragging my heart on the cold granite floor behind me. Unless there was a miracle, the bank wouldn't be my savior. I needed a new plan, and fast.

Before I knew it, I was pulling in front of my childhood home. I pressed the call button and waited.

"Natalie, your mom isn't here." Rosa was better than a guard dog. Her bark into the intercom could scare the toughest of hoodlums, but she didn't scare me. I was impervious to her cartel-like tone.

"Yes, I know, but is there a way to get a hold of her? I have an emergency."

"Health or money?"

It was interesting how those were my only two options. My emergency encompassed a broken heart, a nervous breakdown, a financial disaster, and the ruin of everything I'd come to appreciate, but I was given two to choose from because for a Diamond, those were the only two things that mattered.

"Money."

Only the crackle of static could be heard through the intercom. The silence was like a hundred-pound weight pressing the air from my lungs.

"You'll have to wait for your meeting with your mother on Friday, Natalie."

I swallowed the sob that threatened to burst forth. "What if I had said health? Would you have turned me away then?" I hardly recognized my voice. It cracked and wavered with each word spoken.

"No, of course not. I would have called you a doctor."

"I'm begging you, Rosa." This was the only solution I had. Without Mom's help, I'd lose everything.

"See you Friday, Natalie." There was a click and more silence.

I pulled out of the driveway and down the block before I pulled over and completely lost my shit. Pepper crawled his big body into my lap and licked at my tears. What was I going to do? I looked at my watch. It was almost noon. Time was running out to come up with a solution.

Roland's voice repeated in my head. *You only get one chance with me.*

I'd already used my free pass.

I pushed Pepper from my lap, and my watch caught in his fur. It fell to the floor, and right then I knew what my solution was.

Cartier, here I come.

Chapter 29

NATALIE

No matter how much I begged and pleaded, Cartier's top price was $27,500. It was highway robbery as far as I could figure. They would turn around and resell that watch for forty grand easy, but I didn't have any more time to stand there and haggle—so I took the money.

I was down to less than $100 in my envelope. That left me just over $400 short of what I needed to deliver to the bank before five o'clock. I looked at my wrist and groaned. Now I couldn't even see how little time I had left.

I raced to my cabin to gather anything I had of value. In my closet was a potential gold mine of clothes. I tossed everything with a designer label into a trash bag and rushed back out to the only consignment store I knew.

Riches Rags was a half-hour away. It was three-thirty when I left the cabin. Time was short, but I was determined to succeed.

While the woman at the counter rummaged through the black plastic bag, I tapped my fingers on the counter. My future was coming to an end as this woman divided the items into piles.

"Can we hurry? I have a deadline to meet." My tapping became louder while her pace became slower.

Set Up

"This takes time. These are several years out of fashion." She picked up a Tahari dress and held it up.

Desperation saturated my body, causing beads of sweat to build on my upper lip. "My entire life is a series of fuck-ups, and if I don't get at least $428 for this collection, my life is going to get worse."

She gathered everything and shoved it back into the bags.

My hope descended like a torn kite. She was sending me away with nothing. A tear, followed by another and another, slipped from my eyes. I swiped at them with the back of my hand.

"I can do $450 for the lot. Not a penny more."

My head popped up to see her smiling face.

"Go straighten out your life." She pulled the money from the register and put it in my hand.

"Thank you." I reached across the counter and hugged her. "You're a lifesaver." All I needed to do was get to the bank in less than thirty minutes, and I was golden.

Pepper was waiting patiently in the car for me. "We did it, boy." I ran my hand across his head and revved the engine of the tiny economy car. Hopefully, it had enough oomph to zip through town.

Thirty-five minutes later, I was stuck on Interstate 25 in bumper-to-bumper traffic. I'd missed my deadline by two blocks and ten minutes.

Grief ripped my insides to shreds. I'd lost it all. Roland would never forgive me. Mickey would never forgive me. I would never forgive myself. It all started with a watch and ended with a watch.

By the time I reached the bank, I was despondent. I pounded on the doors and screamed for them to let me in, but the people inside ignored my pleas. They looked at me like I was crazy, then turned their backs.

All that was left was to make the deposit into the night drop box and hope for the best. It was unlikely it would be recorded in time, but at least the effort would be there.

With tear-blurred eyes, I shoved the check and cash into the envelope and wrote in the account number I'd memorized. The drawer opened like a well-oiled piece of machinery, not a squeak, bump, or hang-up of any kind. My life was over, and now the damn drawer worked.

Pepper and I sat in the car until the sun went down. We had no place to go. I couldn't go back to the ranch and face Mickey, and there was no way I could go to Roland's. I wanted my last memory of him to be that kiss he gave me when he told me there was nothing else that could come between us. Boy, was he wrong. Totally screwing up his reputation had created a Grand Canyon of issues that would ruin everything we were together.

After a while, I heard poor Pepper's stomach growl. So, with the last $12 I had to my name, I drove to the pet store and bought him his favorite kibble and a bottle of water. With nowhere to go, I drove to the only neighborhood I knew I wouldn't get mugged in—Cherry Creek. Pulling up to the curb around the bend from my house, I parked under a big sycamore tree.

The police might run the plates, but the car would come up as registered under my mother's name and they would let it sit despite it being nearly a block away from her house.

Tucked into the front seat together, my fur baby and I settled in for the night.

Prison had been my lowest point—until today. At least in prison I had friends and a bunk. Tonight, I was homeless, I had no friends or family, and I was hungry for the first time in my life.

THE RUMBLE of the school bus startled me awake. I rubbed the sleep from my eyes and glanced around. Across the way, the gardeners were unloading their machinery while I let Pepper out to do his business. He chose the Simpson yard, which was fine by me since Mrs. Simpson was the one who called my mom when I snuck out of the house at sixteen. Paybacks were hell.

I stretched the kinks out of my body. My neck and back hurt, but it was my heart that felt like it had been speared with a dull knife that left a jagged bleeding hole.

I missed Roland.

Set Up

I missed my cabin.

I missed my friends.

We climbed back in the car, and before I knew it I was parked in front of the veterinarian clinic. Pepper bounced in his seat and scratched at the door to get out. He was a smart dog to recognize the building where Roland worked. His previous owners were idiots to have given him up. I'd never let him go. All I had left were him and my memories.

My insides twisted in pain. There was nothing I wanted more than to go inside at nine o'clock and flip the switch to the computer and watch it come to life. I would miss making Roland his morning coffee and making his bed—the same bed I made love to him in on countless occasions.

I laid my head on the steering wheel and imagined my replacement. Would she know exactly how to handle the disgruntled patients? Would she adopt the unborn puppies from Terra's Labrador? Would she take my place in every facet of Roland's life?

Sorrow crawled into my throat and choked me. My garbled sounds of distress upset Pepper, and he barked and scratched at the door. Even he couldn't stand me any longer. I wailed out loud at the unfairness of the world, but most of all I wallowed in disappointment. I'd let myself down by letting everyone around me down, and that was worse than anything.

A knock sounded on the window, and I snapped my head to look at who was interrupting my pity party. Big beautiful blue eyes stared at me, and I lost my breath.

Chapter 30

ROLAND

When I saw her parked in front of the clinic, I nearly wept. I'd spent the whole night looking for her. I even pounded on the gate at her mother's house until the housekeeper answered. She told me Natalie had come and gone already. After that, I was lost.

Mickey was the lookout at the ranch while I drove around the city and searched for the proverbial needle in the haystack. It was unlikely I'd find the exact place she had run to, but I had to try. Natalie was everything to me. To give her up would be like giving up oxygen, air, or a vital organ. It would be impossible.

I pounded on the window while she howled louder and louder. It wasn't until Pepper started barking that she lifted her head and took notice of me.

"Unlock the door." I yanked at the handle until it opened. "Where the hell have you been?" My voice wasn't the loving and caring impression I wanted to open with—but I was tired and scared and relieved all at once.

Natalie sucked in unsteady breaths. "I'm sorry, Roland. I never meant to harm you or Mickey. Bad luck follows me around like a dark rain cloud." She wiped her runny nose on her sleeve and proceeded to cry.

Pepper leapt across her lap, exited the car, and danced around me. His whimpers indicated his level of distress.

"We've been searching the city for you since yesterday. What were you thinking?" I reached into the car and pulled her out. She was a mess. Her beautiful brown hair was knotted in the back. Her clothes were wrinkled from head to toe, and she desperately needed a shower. "Holly called every hospital. Megan called every hotel. Where the hell were you?"

She stiffened when I yelled. "Don't yell at me. I'm dirty, hungry, and exhausted. Have you ever slept in a car with a seventy-pound dog who farted all night?"

"I'm sorry." I pulled her to my chest and kissed the top of her head. "I've been worried sick about you."

"I totally screwed things up. One chance was all I got, and I'd used that up weeks ago." She began to cry again.

"What are you talking about?" I wrapped my arm around her shoulders and guided her toward the front door.

"The deposit. It disappeared, and I tried to fix it."

"Natalie, the deposit showed up." I led her to the back and helped her sit on the bed. I began to undress her.

She went on as if she didn't hear me. "I swear I made the deposit before I went to the doctor." She lay on the bed while I shimmied her jeans from her body.

"We know that. The bank called at four o'clock to apologize for the malfunction."

"What malfunction?" She sat upright and cocked her head.

"The drop box drawer came off its track, and the deposit slipped beneath it. When you showed up yesterday, they looked into it and found the problem and the deposit."

"Oh my God, they found it." She collapsed backward and wept.

"Natalie, why didn't you come home to me?" I hardly recognized the desperation in my voice. She'd hurt me deeply by her abandonment.

"How could I?"

"You're supposed to talk to me about these things. That's what couples do. They talk and work things out."

"I couldn't face you knowing I'd destroyed everything you worked for."

I fell to my knees in front of her. "Don't you get it? I could—"

"Love me? Could you still love me if I ruined your business and your reputation?" She lay on the top of our bed, clothed in nothing but grief. "I couldn't live with myself."

I pulled her into a sitting position and held her hands in mine. "Natalie, I do love you. I've loved you since that first day when you fell out of the truck. I didn't want to love you, but you're like a virus that infected my heart."

She pulled her hands from mine and wiped her face. "Did you just accuse me of having a contagious virus?"

I began to laugh. One great thing about Natalie was how she never ceased to surprise me. "No, I told you I love you."

The gloom in her eyes disappeared, and happiness bloomed across her face. "You love me?"

"Yes, and I'll show you how much after you take a shower. You smell like wet dog and kibble."

She bolted from the bed. "We have to open the clinic." She bent down to pick up her dirty jeans.

I tossed them out of her reach. "I've rescheduled all our patients. You are far more important than clients. Now get in that shower before I carry you there myself." I lunged forward and sent her running.

"What about the presentation of the checks?" she asked over her shoulder.

"It's been delayed until this afternoon. Mickey wanted the entire staff of the ranch there. It took a village to pull off what we did, and you're part of that village. Get in the shower, and I'll call Mickey. She's worried sick."

Once I heard the shower start, I dialed Mickey's phone.

"I've got her."

"Where in the hell was she?"

"It doesn't matter. she's back." I ran my hand through my hair and let out the first breath of relief in a day.

"When are you coming to the ranch?"

"Soon. She needs a shower, a meal, and probably a nap."

"Hurry, because she needs to explain how an additional $28,000 made its way into my account."

I hung up and stared at the phone. I knew Natalie had stopped by her mom's house, but the housekeeper had said she'd turned her away. Who does that to a desperate woman?

Minutes later, Natalie walked out of the steamy bathroom wrapped in a towel. I glanced down at her wrist and found it empty. I knew exactly what she had sacrificed for us.

I picked up her wrist and rubbed where her watch would have sat. "Why?"

She looked down and shook her head. "Because I love you."

No more words were exchanged. The rest of the morning was spent making love to the only woman I'd ever loved.

Then I fed her, held her, and loved her some more until we needed to leave.

As we rounded the corner of the ranch, I saw the Channel Five news crew unloading their equipment. I pulled in front of Natalie's cabin, and there sat Mickey on the porch swing. She'd aged five years overnight. We all had.

Once Natalie exited the car, the two women were locked in a hug within seconds.

"I'm so sorry, Natalie. I overreacted. I'm so, so, sorry," Mickey said. She hugged Natalie so tight, the poor woman couldn't take a full breath.

"I'm sorry, too. I deserved every word. I never gave you a reason to trust me."

"Yes, you did, Natalie. I knew your heart, but I thought of myself first."

It was nice to see two women I loved and respected make up. Natalie did have a good heart, and I was glad Mickey recognized it.

Natalie laughed, and it was like sunshine on a gloomy day. "See, I'm rubbing off on you."

"We're rubbing off on each other. Now get your ass into some clean clothes and meet the rest of the ranch hands in front of the stables."

"Yes, ma'am." Natalie gave Mickey a half-assed salute. As much as it would be nice to see, Natalie would never be anyone's subordinate, but she'd probably die trying.

I followed her into the cabin, then into her bedroom, where empty hangers hung in the near-empty closet.

"Your clothes, too?"

She hung her head and nodded. "I was short a bit, so I had to be resourceful."

I pulled a pair of jeans from a hanger and handed her the pink shirt she was wearing the night she propositioned me.

"Have I told you how much I love you?"

"Yes, but keep telling me. It's been a long time since anyone has loved me."

That statement broke my heart. I planned to tell her over and over again until she begged me to stop. Natalie was the most selfless woman I knew.

Under the M and M Ranch sign, we delivered the checks to the recipients in front of hundreds of thousands of viewers. All night long the news footage played, and all I could see was the smile on Natalie's face. I wasn't sure whether it was because she was relieved the situation had been resolved, or whether she smiled because I told her how much I loved her at every opportunity. Either way, she glowed like a hundred-watt light bulb for everyone to see.

Chapter 31

NATALIE

My life had come full circle. I'd stolen a watch for its value to me, then sold it to secure the value of those I loved. Mickey had returned the money, and I turned around and donated it in Pepper's name to the Dumb Friends League. Money had been the most important thing in my existence until I realized nothing carried the value of love.

It was Friday, and I sat at my desk at the veterinarian clinic closing up for the day. I stared at the phone and debated the wisdom of the next call I'd make. Before I lost the courage, I picked up the handset and dialed.

"Mom?"

"Natalie, where are you? You're late." Her tone was corporate crisp.

"I'm not coming." I held my breath and waited to hear all the reasons I was being disrespectful.

"What do you mean, you're not coming?" It was funny to hear her voice catch. I was sure Mom rarely heard the word 'not' in her life unless she was saying it to someone else.

"You were right, Mom. I needed to figure things out for myself.

In all honesty, I'm not ready to deal with the consequences of having money."

"Are you feeling okay, honey? Rosa said you had an emergency."

"Yes, I'm all right. In fact, I'm better than all right." Roland was standing behind me and rubbing my shoulders. "I met a man, and I'm in love with him."

"The veterinarian?" Rosa had been talking again.

"Yes."

"I saw you on the news." Mom paused, and papers shuffled in the background. "I'm proud of you, Natalie."

I couldn't breathe. It had taken Mom twenty-five years to say those words to me. The funny thing was, I didn't need to hear them anymore. In the end, all that mattered was I was proud of myself.

"Thanks. I gotta go."

"Wait. What about a shopping day next week?"

Weeks ago, a shopping date would have sounded awesome. Now it meant time away from the people who mattered most to me. "I have a job, so I'll have to let you know. I have to go. Take care, Mom."

I hung up feeling different. I'd finally found myself. I was Natalie Diamond, and I had four new *C*s down pat: Complicated. Capable. Charitable. Cheerful.

Roland sat on the edge of the desk while I shut down the computer for the night. It was Rick's Roost night, and my life was worth celebrating. Only this time I knew he'd accept any proposition I offered.

"Why did you give up the money when it was so important to you?"

How did I tell him I wasn't giving it up—I was simply delaying the payoff? "I found value in people, not things. Besides, I'm not giving it up. The will says I get my inheritance by the time I'm thirty regardless."

"Oh. That's great."

"Yes, it will be if you and I can come up with a plan on where to use it."

"It's your money, Natalie. Having a small nest egg is important for security. It's why I've spent every penny paying off my dad. I want to build up a nest egg for me…and you…and our future children." He ran his hands through my hair and leaned forward to kiss me.

I loved it when Roland talked about our future. Little did he know how much he'd be getting with me. "Colorado is a community property state, and I'm a valuable Diamond."

"I already told you I'd give you everything I had."

I turned my seat and rolled between his open legs. I held on to his thighs so he didn't fall off the desk. "And I'll share all $38 million with you, too." It didn't help. Roland rocked forward and landed into my lap. "That should offer us some security, don't you think?"

I'd never silenced anyone with my actions, but tonight I'd done it twice.

"You're willing to live my lifestyle for five more years?" he managed to say.

I shrugged. "If you're willing to eat my cooking for five more years, I'm game."

Roland laughed. He grabbed the phone and said, "Call your mother and tell her you changed your mind."

I grabbed the handset and tapped him on the head. "You're awful, but I could love you anyway."

"I'm teasing, and you already love me."

We were late to Rick's Roost because there were several surfaces in the office that hadn't been blessed by our lovemaking yet, and tonight the office chair was scratched off that list.

Chapter 32

NATALIE - THREE MONTHS LATER

"Grab her." I rushed after the black fur ball that whizzed by with my sock in her mouth.

"We can't leave our stuff down. She's already eaten two pairs of my shoes." Roland bent over and swiped up Pepper's daughter.

"You can't complain until she's gobbled up five pairs of your shoes or $15,000 worth." I took her from him and cuddled her under my chin. There was something about the way puppies smelled that made the world perfect.

Terra's Lab had given birth to five puppies—three girls and two boys—and after they were weaned from their mother, they showed up in a basket at the veterinarian clinic. Holly and Megan got the pick of the litter, and Mickey took the runt. She was always a sucker for an underdog. Even Cole broke down and expanded his family with one of the little boys he called John Wayne. Not the most unique name, but it seemed to fit the dog that followed him everywhere.

Mom and I had been establishing a relationship and setting boundaries. I didn't ask for anything, and she didn't put unrealistic expectations on me. We were like strangers meeting for the thousandth time.

Set Up

The shopping date she'd asked for was a success. I forced her out of her comfort zone from Cherry Creek couture to the mall, where she purchased a pair of blue jeans and Toms. "Ranch wear," she called it, and I laughed because she'd be the best-dressed woman on the range.

We met for dinner once a week. I didn't have to sell her on the idea of Roland; she took to him straight away. They conspired together. If it was up to the two of them, I'd be married and pregnant by the time Robyn got out of jail, which was only a few weeks away. However, I was enjoying who I'd become, and I didn't want to rush into another role right away. I'd given up my multiple personalities and focused on being the best me I could.

To assuage my mom's desire for a grandchild, I was giving her this little spitfire of a puppy. She would be good practice for Mom until the real thing materialized. I tied a pink bandana around her neck and nuzzled her soft velveteen ears.

"You're going to love your new home," I whispered. "She's got Prada and Gucci and Michael Kors and Fendi."

A knock rattled the door, and the little yapper started barking. She was perfect for Mom. After a week with this little princess, Mom would think I had been a piece of cake.

Roland swung the door open and let my mother in. "Marla, how are you?" She was dressed in her jeans and canvas slip-ons, but her top was designer all the way.

She walked in, and I watched for her reaction to our small home. The whole place could fit in her kitchen. She didn't say a word, only walked around the space and picked up various knickknacks. She stopped at the picture of Dad in the Beast costume and smiled.

"He always was a beast."

"You loved him, didn't you?"

"More than you can imagine."

I walked to Roland, who was standing by the fireplace watching my mom, and wrapped my arms around his waist. "I can imagine just fine."

Mom stepped over Pepper. He lifted his head to see who was

there, and not showing much interest, he laid it back down on my sock monkey, Bo Bo. I never found the heart to take him back. Pepper needed the comfort of a friend once Roland lopped his nuts off.

"Roland and I saved this one for you." I held out the puppy, and my mom stepped back like I was offering her a poison apple. She was as good with animals as she was with children. I was having second thoughts when she huffed and took the puppy from my hands.

"What am I supposed to do with this?" Mom held the puppy away from her like it was wet, dirty, or stinky.

"Love it, Mom." I pressed the puppy to her chest and watched as she unconsciously pet its head with her chin. "You asked me what changed me." Roland and I walked to the couch and sat next to each other. Mom sat in a side chair and cuddled the puppy. "It was a lot of things, but it started with a dog."

"I told you to get a dog."

My insides warmed at the memory of the day I adopted Pepper. He was like me—alone. "Yes, you did, and it was the best advice you ever gave me. Now it's my turn to give you advice." My mom wasn't much different from who I had been. She was alone. The only people she had were the ones she paid to be there.

"Your life is shit, Mom. You have a company, a great house, and nothing else."

"I have people." She didn't sound indignant the way I imagined she would.

"Name someone you spend time with besides me whom you don't pay."

Her eyes went to the ceiling. She bobbed her head as if she were rummaging through a mental Rolodex and each name came with a nod.

"There's Rosa."

"She doesn't count. She's been on your payroll for three decades."

Mom's head dropped down, and the puppy licked her face. "I've had no one since your father." She sat up taller and lengthened her neck. It was her way of looking beyond her shortcomings.

"Isn't it time? Start with the puppy, Mom. I found there's a lot you can learn from a dog. They are forgiving and unassuming, and they love you no matter what."

"Who are you, and who stole my little girl?"

"I grew up, Mom, and I figured out who I was. I'm a friend, a pet owner, a girlfriend, a volunteer, a cook, and I'm your daughter."

Roland kissed my head and whispered in my ear. "Soon you'll add wife and mother to that list." And I knew he was right.

Kerrick and Mickey were weeks from tying the knot, and the ranch would be a flurry of activity. Robyn was getting released and would come live next door to me. This was my family. They weren't who I was born to, but they were who I chose. Miraculously, my mother was working her way back into my heart, too.

"I'm going to call her Sophie. That sounds like a good puppy name."

"That's perfect, Mom."

"Do you have any advice for me?"

I had a ton of advice. Sell your house. Live in poverty for a week. Volunteer. Do something that makes you feel uncomfortable. Sleep in your car. All of those bits of advice were part of my path and not hers, though. She'd have to forge her own trail, but I did have one piece of advice she should heed.

"Hide your shoes."

NEXT UP IS *SET ON You*

A Sneak Peek at Set On You

Freedom was one step away. I gripped the cold, steel door frame and looked through the window at what could have been. Joe was there—standing—waiting. He had always been my savior, but he no longer belonged to me. I'd given him up the day I almost killed a man.

Officer Ellis' hand hovered over the red button that would release me. "Are you ready?"

Am I? This moment resurrected the memories of every first day of school. Knees shaking. Palms sweating. Heart racing. To navigate was to survive. I'd survived then, and I would survive now.

"One step forward, right?" I looked back at the old man who had been my jailer, mentor, and sometime friend.

Officer Ellis nodded his head. "Yes, Robyn. Move forward, one step at a time. Don't look back." His voice was uncompromising, like a father reprimanding his child. "Don't come back."

I took in a breath of courage and stood tall. At thirty-two, I could do this. "I'm ready." My voice echoed off the lifeless gray walls. I wasn't sure whether I was ready, but it was now or never, and never wasn't an option.

The door buzzed—the lock released—and I was free.

I stumbled through the steel frame and stopped. A memorable scent caught on the wind and pulled me one step at a time down to him. There was safety in familiarity.

My eyes traveled from his brown suede oxfords all the way to the top button of his light blue shirt. The brown hair I'd run my hands through a thousand times hung in messy waves to his collar. He looked good.

"Look at you. Free at last." He stepped forward and put his hands on my shoulders.

Five years without the touch of a man was too long. My heart pounded. But was it truly from the caress of his fingers—or out of the fear of being free?

"It seems like forever."

I hopped off the last step and looked into the warm brown eyes of my ex-fiancé. If things had gone differently, we would have been married and probably on our second or third child. Here he was, still being who he always had been for me—my rescuer.

"It was forever. Can you believe you've been in there for a sixth of your life?" His voice was filled with warmth and regret. "I always thought that sentence was too long for defending yourself."

"I agree, but there seemed to be a disconnect between my truth and Craig Cutter's version of the truth. Putting a man in a wheelchair for life tends to send sympathy to the other side." My voice faded to a hush. "I don't really want to talk about it. It's all in the past, and I've got to think about my future."

He pulled me to a nearby picnic table and sat across from me. Years ago, we would have been thigh to thigh, but that was then. Today was different, although he wasn't looking at me like it was different. He was looking at me in that same possessive way he did from the beginning. The look that said, *You're mine and will always be mine.* But that wedding ring on his finger sang a whole different tune.

"I was thinking of trying to get my job back at Fight for Freedom. You know I always wanted to buy that place."

It was ironic that the martial arts studio I had worked at was all about fighting for freedom, yet my freedom was taken away because I'd fought. I had thought about that night thousands of times. I'd replayed the scenario over and over again. The only alternative wasn't even an alternative. I couldn't let him hurt me, so I fought.

"About that…Sharon sold the dojang. She got too old to run it, and she moved to Florida."

My heart stuttered and stalled. I couldn't swallow. I couldn't breathe. I felt the same as I did the day that judge laid down his gavel and said, *Guilty*.

"Oh, Joe," I said with dazed exasperation. "What am I supposed to do now? That was my fallback plan."

He reached across the worn wooden table and gripped my hand. "You're welcome to stay with me and Tanya. I inherited my grandma's house. There's plenty of room, Tanya isn't expecting our second until November."

The mention of his wife and kids was like a spear through my heart. That was *my* life. I was supposed to live in his grandma's house with my belly large with his child, not some other woman.

"That would never work. What are you going to say? 'Hi honey, I've brought my ex-fiancée to live with us'?"

"Tanya is a good woman. She'd do what's right. She'd do whatever I asked. She might even be able to get a job for you at the supercenter where she used to work."

The idea of living with my ex and his wife seemed like another prison sentence. I refused to be an albatross around his neck, and working at a supercenter was its own particular sort of hell.

I pulled my hand from his and slammed it on the table, lodging a splinter in my palm. "Damn it, I wanted that studio." I picked at the sliver of wood until it was gone, but the spot still stung along with the news of the studio being sold.

"I know you did, but sometimes life has different plans for us." He looked at his watch, and I knew it was time to let him go. In more ways than one.

"I appreciate your offer, but I can't do it."

Every time I'd look at his wife and child, I'd feel something I shouldn't. I'd feel jealousy and regret, and I didn't have time for those emotions. There were five years of my life to make up, and I needed to start now.

"So what will you do?"

"I'll go with plan B. Can you give me a ride?"

"Anywhere you want to go."

That was my Joe. He was a good man who would always be there if I needed him. I pledged to myself right then never to need him again. He had a wife and family waiting at home, and if I didn't let him go, his obsessive need to rescue me would come between them. He'd always been like that. That's why he was here to pick me up instead of Mickey. He wouldn't have it any other way.

"Let's go."

I stood from the bench and made my way toward his car. Now that my dream was gone, there was only one place in the world that might stand a chance of feeling like home and only one group of people who might be family.

The car idled in the parking area of the ranch. I leaned over and gave Joe a hug, but he pulled me in for an awkward kiss on the cheek. I wormed out of the embrace and pulled the half-empty duffle bag he had kept for me all these years from the back seat. It held everything I had in the world. I gave him one last glance before I headed up the walkway toward the big ranch house.

I stood on the top step and took in my surroundings. There was the big house, a barn, and a huge building of some sort, probably the arena Mickey had told me about. In the distance, eight cabins sat side by side, looking like a brochure for summer camp.

This place was different from what I imagined, but it was full of the people who got Mickey through her prison experience. Maybe they could help me, too.

When I got to the front door, I could hear the girls talking. A metal plaque hung from the wood panel that read *It's open, come on in*. Another below it read *Clean the shit from your boots*.

I walked into the main house to find Mickey and the girls feverishly plotting over her upcoming wedding.

"No, I think the tables should be here, and the bar here."

A Sneak Peek at Set On You

Natalie leaned over a piece of paper that had been written on and erased so many times, there were holes in it.

Holly sat back and rubbed her expanding belly, but no one noticed that I'd entered.

"Hey," I said, but they were so caught up in what they were doing, they didn't hear me. Desperate times required desperate measures. At thirty-two, I was physically fit. I could bench press two and a half times my weight and run hurdles better than a woman ten years younger. Not wanting to remain invisible, I took three long strides and hopped onto the center of the table.

"Attention, bitches! Your favorite troublemaker has arrived!"

Finally, they noticed me, and before I could say another word, I was pulled off the table and forced into the center of a group hug.

"Why didn't you say something?" Mickey pulled me all to herself and squeezed me tight.

"I did, but something must happen to your ears when you plan a wedding. Deaf as a doorknob, the lot of you." I looked at the paper and shook my head. "The biggest dilemma should not be where the gift table goes, ladies. Have I taught you nothing?"

I pulled the page toward me and started writing. On the opposite side of the arena from the door, I wrote *Male Model Auction*. Next to that, I drew a long rectangle and labeled it *Open Bar*.

Megan looked at the makeshift map and laughed. "Leave it to Raging Robyn to spend two minutes in front of the map and figure it all out."

'Raging Robyn' was what the guards called me because I didn't take shit from anyone. No one touched me or told me anything. Most women were in jail for drugs or petty crimes. A few murdered their lying, cheating husbands, but not one of them had the skill to snap a neck with one move. That particular talent was mine alone. No one bothered me, and they didn't bother my friends either.

Natalie's blue eyes widened. "Are we having a male model auction? I'm not sure Roland will like that."

"Oh, my God, are you all dick whipped?"

The girls looked at each other and nodded. Every single one of them was in love. I was happy for them, but I'd be lying if I said I wasn't a little jealous. Five damn years I'd given up, all because some asshole had wanted to rob the studio. While I sat in prison, everyone else had moved on with their lives.

Mickey grabbed a six-pack of beer from the refrigerator and handed a can to everyone but Holly. She got a bottle of water.

I flipped the metal tab and watched the bubbles threaten to spill, but they rose and fell.

"Here's to family," Mickey said and raised her drink.

We all raised our cans in salute. I took a long draw of the cold beer and relished the tickle of the carbonation as it slid down my throat. I licked my lips, savoring the taste of freedom. Maybe this wasn't going to be as bad as I thought.

Get a free book.

Go to www.authorkellycollins.com

Other Books by Kelly Collins

The Second Chance Series

Set Free

Set Aside

Set in Stone

Set Up

Set on You

The Second Chance Series Box Set

The Boys of Fury Series

Redeeming Ryker

Saving Silas

Delivering Decker

The Boys of Fury Boxset

About the Author

International bestselling author of more than thirty novels, Kelly Collins writes with the intention of keeping love alive. Always a romantic, she blends real-life events with her vivid imagination to create characters and stories that lovers of contemporary romance, new adult, and romantic suspense will return to again and again.

For More Information
www.authorkellycollins.com
kelly@authorkellycollins.com

Acknowledgments

Where do I start? When I wrote the first book, Set Free, I had no idea where this series would go. I knew I had five ex-convicts, and a bunch of Irish McKinleys along with one sexy veterinarian and a bunch of ranch hands.

The first book was finished, and I wasn't sure I had an audience for the series. I considered leaving it as a stand alone until several people in my street team asked when book two would be released.

If you like The Second Chance Series, thank the men and women of Kelly Collins' Book Nook who demanded I continue the series.

A big thanks to my priority reader team, beta readers like Karen and Leeann, and Tammy, you are part of a team that made it possible for this book to be what it is.

Most important, I want to thank you, the reader, who have traveled this journey with me. I write for you and I'm grateful you read my words.

Hugs,
Kel

Printed in Great Britain
by Amazon